"Hello?"

Libby entered the nearly empty kitchen, remembering the many times she'd been here in the past—usually when Kade's dad was gone.

The hammering stopped abruptly and Kade appeared at the end of the hall, wearing a sweaty T-shirt that clung to his chest, outlining his muscles. Libby swallowed and recalled her role. Civil acquaintance.

She cleared her throat. "Uh, hi," she said, suddenly aware that "civil acquaintance" was going to be a lot more difficult than "angry ex." Anger felt safe, protected her from having to acknowledge that she still found Kade ridiculously attractive. She could close her eyes and remember how it felt to smooth her hands over his muscles, feel his lips on her—

"Hi," he echoed. For a moment they stared at each other, his questioning hazel eyes meeting her cautious blue ones.

Libby squared her shoulders. "I came to tell you that I changed my mind. I will go with you to find Blue."

His expression didn't change. "Why?"

Because I need to prove to both of us that there will never be anything between us again.

Dear Reader,

Imagine what it would be like to have the most important person to you, your soul mate, betray you. This is what happened to Libby Hale when her childhood friend and fiancé, Kade Danning, left her to marry another woman. Libby is not the forgiving kind, so she has no intention of renewing any kind of relationship with Kade when he comes back, divorced and in the process of rebuilding his life, ten years later. Unfortunately for her, Kade has other plans.

Libby was first featured in *The Cowboy's Redemption* as the hero's best friend. She was an irreverent, straight-talking, no-nonsense woman, and so much fun to write that I knew I had to explore her character further. Thus *Cowboy Comes Back* was born, a story of second chances—for a man, a woman and a horse.

I love to hear from readers. Please e-mail me at jeanniewrites@gmail.com or visit my Web site at www.jeanniewatt.com.

Happy reading,

Jeannie Watt

COWBOY COMES BACK
Jeannie Watt

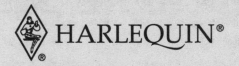

HARLEQUIN®

TORONTO • NEW YORK • LONDON
AMSTERDAM • PARIS • SYDNEY • HAMBURG
STOCKHOLM • ATHENS • TOKYO • MILAN • MADRID
PRAGUE • WARSAW • BUDAPEST • AUCKLAND

Recycling programs
for this product may
not exist in your area.

ISBN-13: 978-0-373-78321-2

COWBOY COMES BACK

ABOUT THE AUTHOR

Jeannie Watt lives with her husband in an isolated area of northern Nevada, and teaches junior-high science in a town forty miles from her home. She lives off the grid in the heart of ranch country and considers the battery-operated laptop to be one of the greatest inventions ever. When she is not writing, Jeannie likes to paint, sew and feed her menagerie of horses, ponies, dogs and cats. She has degrees in geology and education.

Books by Jeannie Watt

HARLEQUIN SUPERROMANCE

1379–A DIFFICULT WOMAN
1444–THE HORSEMAN'S SECRET
1474–THE BROTHER RETURNS
1520–COP ON LOAN
1543–A COWBOY'S REDEMPTION

Don't miss any of our special offers. Write to us at the following address for information on our newest releases.

Harlequin Reader Service
U.S.: 3010 Walden Ave., P.O. Box 1325, Buffalo, NY 14269
Canadian: P.O. Box 609, Fort Erie, Ont. L2A 5X3

I've never met an Ellen I haven't liked. In fact, one of the Ellens I like very much mentioned that Ellens in fiction are always nice friends or neighbors. Never villains. I decided to employ the rule of opposites and do something about that.

This book is dedicated to all the nice Ellens in my life— fellow Superromance author Ellen Hartman, fellow teacher Ellen Too, and my former high-school classmate and college roommate, with whom I threw vanilla wafers at the neighbor's window, Ellen Swanson.

CHAPTER ONE

ROUGH OUT JEANS. RIDE with the Best.

Until you screw up, that is.

Kade Danning grimaced as he walked past his own self-assured face smiling from an old advertisement still tacked outside the local feed co-op. Sort of a Kade Danning memorial. Damn, but he'd been cocky back then.

Well, he wasn't feeling so cocky now. And he wouldn't be posing for photos or endorsing jeans again anytime in the near future. Nope. He'd screwed up that deal royally.

Only one pickup sat in the parking lot—a fancy, shiny red one with duallies and running lights. So there was a chance the store would be empty soon. Good. He wanted to talk to Zero Benson alone.

Earlier that day, he'd driven the fifty miles from Otto, Nevada, to the larger town of

Wesley, where he'd dropped off an application at the personnel office of the Lone Eagle Mine. He'd also put in a general application at the Wesley employment office and then, on the way home, he'd decided to stop at the feed store. Zero would know of any ranch work that might see him through until he was able to find something more permanent.

Zero was standing behind the barn-wood counter when Kade walked into the store, deep in conversation with a man Kade didn't know—a money guy, from the looks of it. Creased Wranglers, neat white shirt, neat white mustache. His hat alone would pay for the new fridge Kade had a feeling he'd need to buy to replace the monstrosity in his father's house.

Neither man had noticed his arrival, so Kade hung about at the back of the store, near the racks of halters and bridles, scanning the want ads tacked to the wall while he waited for the conversation to end. Horses for sale. Tractor services. Shoeing. Nothing in the Help Wanted.

"Have you tried his brother?" Zero asked the guy.

"I don't like his brother," the man stated adamantly.

"Then I don't know what—" Kade glanced up when Zero abruptly stopped speaking, and he saw the older man's mouth gape open. "Well, hell's bells!" Zero said, lumbering out from behind the counter and sidestepping a pallet of feed bags. "Kade. How are you?"

"Good," Kade lied. Zero's face was rounder and more wind-burned than the last time he'd seen him ten years ago, but other than that, his former part-time employer looked the same. He might even have been wearing the same overalls and flannel shirt.

"So are you back or just visiting?" Zero asked, clapping Kade hard on the shoulder.

"I'm working on my dad's house, getting it ready to sell."

The man with the white mustache frowned at Kade, obviously trying to place him.

"This is *Kade Danning*," Zero explained to the man. "Kade, Joe Barton. Mr. Barton bought the Boggy Flat ranch last year."

"Zephyr Valley ranch," Barton corrected him.

Zero made a hoity-toity face. "Like he said. Hey, you want a job?"

Kade's stomach dropped. Was it that obvious? Had Zero heard things that Kade hoped weren't common knowledge? The IRS trouble had been much publicized, but he'd tried to keep the fact that he was dead broke to himself. "I, uh…"

"Mr. Barton has some colts to start and he can't get 'em in to Will Bishop."

Joe Barton appeared none too thrilled at Zero's suggestion. "Zero—"

Kade jumped in to save them both further embarrassment. He'd forgotten Zero's habit of saying whatever popped into his mind. "Can't," he said with a shake of his head. "I'm going to be busy working on the place. I want it on the market by the end of June and my daughter's coming in July, so…sorry."

And then he beat it out of there. He'd come back later or call to see if Zero had heard of any ranch work—preferably not on the Barton spread, since Barton hadn't seemed all that impressed with him. But the guy had to be loaded if he'd bought the Boggy Flat. The ranch was huge.

"Don't you know who that *was?*" he heard Zero ask as he escaped through the open door.

Was. The word summed up Kade's life well.

LIBBY HALE CURSED under her breath as she drove by the Danning ranch early Friday morning and saw that the yard lights were on again.

As if she didn't have enough trouble in her life without Kade showing up.

But she would *not* let his presence get to her. He wasn't the reason she was having trouble sleeping.

The road from Otto to Wesley was a straight shot through the desert to the northeast, over one mountain range and then down into the adjoining sage-covered valley. Libby drove it at least four times a week, sometimes five, depending on the length of her workdays. Usually she traveled on autopilot, planning her schedule, but today she focused on the road, refusing to think about anything but her driving.

There was one car in the Bureau of Land Management parking lot when Libby pulled in. Ellen Vargas's highly polished Lexus SUV. Libby parked at the opposite end of the lot and sat for a moment, staring at her boss's Lexus and wondering how long it would be before she came to work and the damned thing wouldn't be there.

It was no secret that Ellen Vargas would move on as soon as she could, following an upwardly mobile career track in government. Libby only hoped Ellen didn't do too much damage before that happened.

The building was dimly lit when Libby walked in, since Francine, the receptionist, wasn't at work yet. The only bright light spilled out of Ellen's open office door. Libby would have loved to tiptoe by, but it wasn't her style, so she said, "Morning," as she passed on the way to her office.

"Good morning, Libby. Do you have a minute?"

Wonderful.

Libby reversed course and stepped into Ellen's office. When Glen had been there, the manager's office had been pleasantly cluttered. Now it looked like a page out of *House Beautiful.* A vase with a single exotic flower stood on the corner of the government-issue desk, making Libby wonder where on earth Ellen had managed to find an orchid in Wesley—if it was, indeed, a real orchid and not a silk replica. But if it was a silk replica, it was very realistic…. Libby had an urge to poke at it, to see if it was genuine, but she didn't think Ellen would appreciate that. Maybe she'd come back later, while her boss was mustering the troops.

"How long have you been a wild horse specialist, Libby?"

Ellen already knew the answer, just as she knew everything about everyone who worked for her. She'd done her homework. But since she asked, Libby answered, thus demonstrating that she was a team player, cooperative, responsive and accountable.

"Three years."

"And before that you were a range conservationist?"

"Yes." She'd hired on as a range con, never suspecting that the wild horse position—her dream job—would open up four years later, right when she was poised to slip into the position. Sometimes things did fall into place.

"You seem to enjoy your work."

"Yes."

She would also enjoy it if Ellen got to the point. The woman's highly polished gold-rimmed glasses glinted as she tilted her head slightly. Behind the glasses her eyes were perfectly made-up. Liner, shadow, mascara. How was it that she could apply cosmetics so well, so early in the morning? Libby could barely see when she got up, much less apply eyeliner with precision. And she could only imagine what she'd have to go through to make her long curly hair approach Ellen's blond lacquered perfection.

"I've skimmed the past few years' records and—" Ellen tapped her pencil on the desk "—I don't understand the procedure with these animals that people gain title to months after the official adoption period has passed."

"Those are the leppies."

The glasses slid down Ellen's nose a fraction of an inch as she dropped her chin. "The leppies?"

"Orphans."

"I see."

But she didn't see—it was obvious. And she would be looking into the matter— equally obvious. This was what happened when people from Florida were put in charge of operations in the Nevada desert and vice versa—there was a huge learning curve and an enhanced propensity for poor decision making. When Ellen's ego was factored in... Oh, yes. This was going to be a fine year.

"There are people who will take in orphans caught in the gathers and care for them. In return they get title to the foals once they're old enough to freeze-brand."

"And they pay nothing."

"Do you have any idea what mare-milk replacer costs?"

"Is this common practice?"

"It is here."

Ellen inhaled in a way that indicated perhaps she'd heard those words too often since she'd come to work in the Wesley field office. "All right. Thank you for explaining. We'll meet again more formally after I've had a chance to go over all the files."

"Just tell me when." Libby patted the door frame and then escaped. "Sheesh," she muttered as she unlocked the office she shared with Stephen, the range con who'd taken her place when she became a wild horse specialist.

She sat at her desk without bothering to turn on the lights and stared at the blank computer screen, surprised to realize that even though she should have been steaming after the conversation with Ellen, she was wondering, instead, just how long Kade would be in Otto. How long it'd be until she ran into him. And why she, who generally welcomed confrontation, didn't feel quite ready for that day.

KADE STEPPED OUT of the living quarters of his horse trailer, which was parked next to the ancient stone barn, and started across the weed-choked driveway to the house. Three nights on the property and he still couldn't bring himself to sleep in his old bed. He didn't know if he ever would.

The sun was barely over the mountains and he had a full day ahead of him in the house he hated. But it was also his daughter's ninth birthday, so at least he could end the day on a positive note by calling her and seeing how she liked the present he'd mailed a few days ago.

He crossed the weathered porch, which echoed under his boots, and opened the kitchen door. Then he stood for a moment, one hand on the worn doorjamb as he steeled himself for the day ahead, taking in the scarred tile floor and the decrepit kitchen appliances. The big enamel sink, where he'd washed a million dishes while his father yelled at him. The fridge that contained who knew what.

No one had come in to clean after his father had died. There'd been no funeral, no memorial, no will. And since the property had been in legal limbo at the time, Kade had made the final arrangements over the phone. It had seemed cold, but it was what his father had wanted. No funeral. No contact with his son.

Even when Kade had become a world champion bronc rider, his father had wanted nothing to do with him. And now Kade wanted nothing to do with anything that reminded him of his father—including his father's ranch.

But he had tons of work ahead of him before he could sell. As Marvin the Realtor had pointed out when Kade had first contacted him, ramshackle houses, sagging fences and weedy pastures were not all that easy to market. Marvin might be new in the real-estate business, but he recognized the obvious.

Kade stepped into the kitchen. Number one, the fridge, which he'd avoided for the first few days while he'd concentrated on the other rooms. One look inside and he resigned himself to buying a new one. Not only was the appliance more than twenty years old, it was filled with an assortment of overgrown and dried-up…stuff that definitely qualified as biohazards. He shut the door, considered duct-taping it shut so that whatever was inside wouldn't come creeping out during the night, and made arrangements over the phone for a new one.

By the time he was done, his gut was at boot level, but Marvin had also said that showing a house without decent appliances was not a smart idea. Trouble was, right now he didn't have a lot of money. And what he did have was dwindling fast.

Zero had promised to call if he heard of any work, when Kade had finally gotten hold of him the night before, but there was nothing at the moment. It was kind of the way Kade's luck had been running for the past five or six years, so he shouldn't have been surprised.

Cleaning went better while he was focused on his lack of finances. The memories didn't bite at him every time he opened a door or found something that reminded him of his teen years. He still hadn't ventured into his dad's room, but he'd pretty well gutted the living room and kitchen. He had his dad's stock trailer loaded with stuff that he would take to the dump or to Goodwill. He didn't want any reminders. He just hoped the tires on the trailer held out, because he didn't want to replace them.

Kade finally left the house, exhausted, at six o'clock for his dump run. But he waited until eight to call his daughter, as per his ex-wife Jillian's instructions—after Maddie's birthday party, before bedtime.

"Hi, Daddy," she said when she came on the phone, and as usual Kade felt a pull deep in his chest at the sound of her voice. "Let me tell you *everything* that's been happening...."

Kade smiled and settled back in the lawn chair next to his horse trailer, propping his feet on the fender. "Shoot, kid."

Maddie prattled on for at least five minutes, ending with, "And then Mike took us to the game, and after that, pizza."

"Sounds excellent."

"It was the best birthday ever," Maddie concluded. "I wish you could have been here," she added, but it sounded like a polite afterthought.

"Me, too." Jillian and Mike had been married for two years. They had year-old twins Maddie adored, and they were raising Maddie in a much more stable home than the one he'd provided, being on the road with the rodeo for a good part of the year.

Which was the problem. Jillian was overcompensating for that earlier unpredictability by insisting that every aspect of Maddie's life had to be stable. Therefore, she didn't want Maddie visiting Kade for the two months he was supposed to have her during the summer. It hadn't been such a problem when they'd all lived in Boise, but once Jillian and Mike had moved to Elko a year ago, it had become an issue.

"It'll upset her routine. She has softball and dance...." Jillian hadn't come out and said it, but Kade knew she wished he would disappear so that Maddie would have only one father—Mike.

"I'm going to horse camp this summer," Maddie announced. "It's my big present from Mike and Mom. Camp lasts for almost a whole month! Three and a half weeks!"

Kade felt his jaw tighten. "What month is that?"

"July."

Which would make her two-month summer visit with him difficult, if not impossible. He wondered when Jillian had planned to break the news to him. And why it was all right for Maddie to be at a camp with strangers for three and a half weeks, but not with her own father.

"It's in Boise," Maddie continued, "so Grandma will be close in case I get homesick. And Shandy may be able to go, too!"

"Sounds cool." Kade had tried to sound sincere.

"I really like the necklace you sent me." Maddie happily jumped topics.

"Do you?"

"Yeah. Mom says I have to save it for good."

"I want you to wear it, Maddie." He tried not to contradict Jillian, figuring it was important that his daughter not sense hostility between the two of them, but this was getting ridiculous. Oh, yes. He and Jillian would be talking soon. "That's why I bought it."

"Okay. I'll ask Mom if I can have it back. She's keeping it safe for me."

Kade decided to change the subject before he exploded. "I'm getting another horse."

"Really? I hated it when you sold Blaze...."

Kade and Maddie talked about horses for several minutes more, the one love they shared that Jillian didn't butt into, and then he heard Jillian announce it was bedtime.

"You better go, kiddo."

"Yeah. Thanks for calling, Dad. I'll see you tomorrow!"

The line clicked dead before he could say goodbye. Kade hung up feeling depressed. His daughter was growing up fast. So fast he was afraid that before he got his act together she'd be gone. And if Jillian had her way he'd never really get to be part of her life, just the bearer of gifts on her birthday and at Christmas. That wasn't the role he wanted— or deserved.

The only times he hadn't been part of Maddie's life were when he'd been on the road rodeoing and making a living, and during the dark months after Jillian had left him, when he'd started drinking too much and messing up his life. Other than that, he'd been there, trying his best to do things right, to be a decent dad.

Hell, he *was* a decent dad—stellar by comparison to his own father. He walked over to the door of the trailer and stared out across the field at Libby's place. He'd given up a lot to be a dad, but it was a sacrifice he'd had to make. He'd screwed up and he'd had to do the right thing.

His only regret was Libby.

CHAPTER TWO

THE MORE TIME KADE spent trying to fix the house, the more things he found wrong with it. Cracked moldings, saggy hinges, leaky plumbing, holes in the walls. Problems he needed to remedy if he wanted to hook a buyer for the property. He was on his second trip to the hardware store that day, trying to find a coupling for repairing the bathroom sink and knowing full well he'd probably discover some other part he needed, just as soon as he got home. Plumbing was like that.

"I heard you were back." Startled, Kade looked up to see Jason Ross standing a few feet away, next to some big rolls of copper tubing. From his dark expression, it was clear Jason wasn't there to welcome Kade.

"Hey, Jason. How are you?" Once upon a time they'd been friends, had ridden rodeo together in high school, but Jason didn't appear to be all that friendly now. His lean face was set in harsh, unfamiliar lines.

"I'm good," Jason said flatly. "Fixing up your dad's place?"

"Hoping to get it on the market by the end of next month." Kade shifted his weight as he spoke and waited for what had to be coming. There was a stretch of uncomfortable silence and then Jason finally got to the point.

"Have you seen Libby?"

"Not yet."

"Maybe it'd be best if you didn't."

Direct. Very Jason-like. And uncalled-for.

"I don't think you have a lot of say in the matter," Kade said, twisting the PVC coupling he was holding in his hands.

Jason glanced behind him to see if anyone was within hearing range before he turned back and said, "I'm her friend, so yeah, I do have a say. You don't need to shove your way back into her life. You did enough damage the last time."

"If I want to see Libby, I'll damned well see her." Kade spoke slowly and deliberately. He wasn't about to clear what he did or didn't do with Jason. "And believe it or not, hurting Libby was the last thing I ever wanted to do."

"You failed," Jason said shortly. He gave a curt nod, then turned and headed back the way he'd come. Conversation over. Warning delivered.

Kade watched his former friend disappear around the end of the aisle before attempting to turn his thoughts back to plumbing. But it was damned hard to concentrate with adrenaline pumping through him.

He glanced at his watch. He had to drive to Elko to pick up Maddie for their weekend together and if he didn't get going, he'd be late. Another black mark against him in Jillian's book. As it was, she would act as if she were sending her baby into a war zone or somewhere equally dangerous when she handed Maddie over, and Kade would try not to react since Maddie was so observant. He didn't want her picking up more bad parental vibes. The divorce had been hard on her and it wasn't until Mike had come into the picture that Maddie had settled—possibly because Jillian was finally happy.

Kade's cell phone rang as he walked to the truck with a bag of plumbing parts that he hoped would cover all eventualities. He waited until he'd unlocked the door to answer, catching the call on the sixth ring, just before it went into voice mail.

"Kade. I think I may have something." Sheri Mason sounded excited.

Kade frowned. "What do you mean, *have something?* You aren't supposed to be looking for anything."

"Yeah, yeah, yeah. It's not definite, but Rough Out is talking about a campaign with an indestructibility theme. You know—no matter what you do to them, how much you beat them up, these jeans can take it. And they want big-name veteran rodeo stars. Guys who have been beat up but keep on going. You fit the bill."

"I'm unreliable." Which was why Rough Out had fired him in the first place. Apparently they wanted their spokesman to be sober and show up for work.

"And I'm good. I think we have a shot at this."

Kade couldn't handle another yo-yo experience. The old *yes, they want you…no, they don't.* He'd had his hopes dashed a few too many times of late.

"Tell you what, Sheri. You do what you think is best here. If you want to pursue this, great, but I'm telling you not to waste your time if you think this *is* a waste of time."

"Sweetheart, if I thought you were a waste of time I would have stopped being your agent when I stopped dating you. I'll keep you posted."

"Don't." Kade spoke before thinking. But it was the truth. "Just tell me if I make the short list, all right?"

"You got it. Bye, love."

Kade flipped the phone shut and stuck it in his pocket.

"AND THEN KADE told Jason he could do as he damned well pleased where Libby was concerned. I was right on the other side of the aisle weighing nails. I heard him."

"Well, don't announce it to the world, you fool. That could affect the odds."

The men's voices were loud enough to be heard at the door when Libby opened it, but they fell silent as soon as she stepped inside the almost empty bar and waited a moment for her eyes to adjust. She found it amazing that anyone was in a bar at 7:00 a.m., but Nevada was a twenty-four-hour state and some people had developed unusual circadian cycles. The only reason she was there at such a ridiculous hour was that she'd picked up a package at the Wesley post office as a favor to the owner and was delivering it on her way to do her Saturday-morning shopping.

Libby set her jaw and went up to the bar. It was dumb to let the dealings of two morons upset her, since nothing happened in Otto without a flurry of betting amongst the local ne'er-do-wells. Marriage, divorce, weight loss. Everything that happened had a few bucks riding on it. Libby was not the betting kind and generally ignored such activity. But she'd never been the subject of it before.

"So, what *are* the odds?" she asked Julie, the bartender, setting down the box she carried.

"For which bet?" Julie idly pushed the lank brown hair that had escaped her up-do away from her face.

"Which bet?" Libby did her best not to look outraged. She normally didn't become outraged unless she was dealing with bureaucracy or fuel prices. "How many are there?"

Julie shrugged her thin shoulders, making her tank top slide off to one side, before reciting in a monotone, "Rekindled romance, eight to one. One night of passion, even money."

Libby's eyes widened still more.

"And I'm betting *against* one-night stand, so if you do have one—" Julie made a please-cooperate face as she pulled her top back into place "—don't tell anyone. Okay?"

Libby slapped her palm on the bar, then headed for the door. She had had enough.

Kade would do as he damned well pleased where she was concerned? She'd see about that.

Libby felt remarkably calm as she got into her truck and drove to Kade's ranch. They were about to get a few things straight, she and Kade. It was time to meet face-to-face. Get it over with, rather than dying a thousand deaths wondering when she was going to bump into him. Libby wasn't one to avoid confrontation, but she'd been avoiding this one, which made her feel weak. Time to change that.

Kade's truck was parked under a scraggly tree at the edge of the yard, but Libby somehow knew the house was empty before her knuckles touched the rough wood of the kitchen door. No one answered, so she peered through the curtainless window in the door. The kitchen was empty—the fridge was gone, the counters were bare and the table and chairs were nowhere in sight.

"Lib—"

She almost had a heart attack when Kade spoke from behind her. She whirled around, angry at her reaction and ready to take it out on him, fair or not. But she hadn't counted on the impact of seeing him standing there, tall and lean. The same, yet different. And still as sexy as hell, if one went by appearances alone.

He had a bad case of bed head, his wheat-colored hair sticking out in several directions, and a thick growth of stubble on his chin and jaw—which seemed even more chiseled than before. Standing barefoot on the gravel, he rubbed one hand self-consciously over his head as he apparently waited for her to say something.

When she didn't speak, mainly because she was fighting back memories triggered by his disheveled appearance, he asked, "What are you doing here?"

She looked him up and down, collecting

herself, taking refuge in anger once again. Much safer there. "Where'd you come from?"

He pointed at his horse trailer. "I don't sleep in the house." He was more muscular than he'd been ten years ago, and there was a new scar on the side of his face, curving close to his left eyebrow. Probably the result of that bronc stomping him just before he'd won his second world title. Libby had read about it in the papers and had been bitter enough at the time to have rooted for the horse.

"Daddy?"

Libby's eyes jerked toward the trailer in time to see a girl with a mop of tousled blond hair poke her head out the door.

"It's just a friend, Maddie. I'll be back in a minute."

But the girl had already jumped to the ground and was heading toward them, the silvery shapes on her pink pajamas glinting in the early sun.

This is the child. Kade's child. The reason Libby had discovered that he'd been sleeping with someone else while she'd been hundreds of miles away, working on her degree. The girl came closer and hugged Kade's waist, staring at Libby as she leaned against her father.

Reality sucked. It really did. Libby liked it better when the kid was just some faceless entity, not a flesh-and-blood little girl with Kade's hazel eyes.

"This is Madison," Kade said, and it was easy to see that he did not want Libby to do anything to upset his daughter. As if she would—it wasn't the kid's fault that Kade couldn't keep his fly zipped. Libby forced the corners of her mouth up when all she really wanted to do was escape. "Hi, Madison."

"Hi," the girl said, obviously as curious as Libby was uncomfortable. "You can call me Maddie. All Dad's friends do."

Libby didn't know how to deal with this. None of her combative strategies applied here, and this was obviously not the time to do battle.

"I've got to go," she said, brushing past Kade and his daughter, not caring what either of them thought. She needed to regroup.

Libby couldn't remember the last time she'd turned tail and run. Even when Kade had come to her to confess that he'd gotten a woman pregnant and had to do the right thing, she'd held her ground—mainly out of shock, but she'd held it. Kade had been the one to leave.

She was startled when Kade caught up with her as she reached the bumper of her truck.

"Why'd you come, Lib?"

She glanced over his shoulder to see his daughter mounting the steps to the trailer, shooting one last curious glance their way before disappearing inside.

I came because I wanted to get this reunion over with and move on. I wanted to prove to myself that I've been losing sleep over nothing.

But the words wouldn't come. So she hedged.

"They're taking bets about us at the bar."

"Of course they are. You must have known that would happen."

"Listen, Kade. I live a quiet life now. I don't like to be stared at or gossiped about." She managed to hold his gaze as she spoke.

"Since when? You've never cared what anyone thought."

So much for hedging. "I cared what you thought, for all the good it did me."

"I wanted to get married," he said in a voice so low it was almost a growl. "You were the one who demanded more time. You were the one who said we should make sure before we took the big step."

"I didn't think you'd be sleeping with other women, or raising families with them."

"It happened. I wasn't going to walk out on her."

Her. Libby was surprised that she felt a stab of jealousy. She tilted her head back. "You did the right thing. For *her.*"

"I had no choice."

"No," she admitted, "you didn't." He couldn't have come back to her when he was having a baby with someone else. She wouldn't have *had* him back.

"I still don't know why you're here," he said.

"You want to know why I'm here? Because, regardless of what you think, I don't appreciate being bet on and talked about. I'd prefer not to have people watching us to see what's going to happen next, like we're some kind of reality show."

"What are you talking about?" he asked with a perplexed scowl.

"You told Jason you'd do as you damned well pleased where I'm concerned."

Kade hooked his thumb in his belt and regarded her for another long moment. "I didn't mean it the way it sounds."

"Well, it's what someone heard and it's affecting the odds."

"Libby…"

The way he said her name sent a small tingle through her body. And it pissed her off. "Just keep your distance and I'll keep mine. I think you owe me that much, Kade." She opened the truck door, putting a barrier between them. "It was nice to meet your daughter."

Libby got in and turned the key, throwing the truck into Reverse almost as soon as the engine fired and leaving Kade standing in the driveway.

Talk about plans being derailed. She'd come on the offensive and had left on the retreat. That wasn't the way she normally did things, but it was the way she'd done them today.

And she didn't know why.

Libby slowed as she approached a corner. No, she did know why, and it was more than the kid being there. Seeing Kade had thrown her completely off-kilter. No matter how many times she'd told herself that she'd moved on over the past few years, it was obvious now that she'd been wrong.

She was still pissed off at Kade. And she still hated him for what he'd done.

"WHO'S THAT LADY, DAD?" Maddie asked as soon as Kade opened the trailer door.

Try as he might, Kade couldn't say "no one."

"We grew up together," he said as he shut the door behind him. He glanced into the mirror that was visible through the door of the small bathroom and he grimaced. He looked like a derelict. He didn't usually sleep this late, but Maddie had been wound up the night before and she'd talked well into the small hours before he convinced her to slide her folding door shut and get some sleep.

"Why's she mad at you?"

"Because I hurt her feelings once." He headed for the coffeepot.

"A long time ago?"

"Yep."

"And she's *still* mad?" Maddie blinked as she asked the question.

Kade poured coffee into a mug, took a sip. Then another. "Some people stay mad a long time, sweetie."

"I don't."

"You're lucky. Come on," he said, jerking his head toward the stove. "I'll make breakfast. You set the table."

"Pancakes?"

"You bet."

Maddie set the tiny fold-out table while Kade whipped up pancakes from a mix and started cooking dollar-size cakes in a cast-iron frying pan. Maddie loved the trailer because everything was small. She thought it was like living in a dollhouse, whereas Kade was getting a bona fide case of cabin fever after only a week. But he wouldn't sleep in the house. He hated the feel of the place, could still feel his father's malevolent presence.

"I want to see the blue horse before I go."

"He's not really blue, Maddie," Kade replied as he flipped pancakes. His nerves were still humming from his encounter with Libby. She hadn't changed much. She was still full of fire. Still beautiful with all that long curly hair and those flashing blue eyes.

And she had obviously been unnerved by meeting Maddie.

Not that there was a chance in hell that her feelings toward his child would matter one way or the other. Libby was not, by nature, the trusting kind, and he'd done more than break her trust. He'd decimated it. But she'd also done a number on him, too, when she'd told him she wasn't sure she wanted to get married.

"I know he's not *really* blue," Maddie replied airily, bringing his attention back to her. "He's a blue roan. He has black and white and gray hairs mixed, and it looks like he's blue."

Maddie had had blue roans on the brain ever since Kade had told her about Blue, the stud his grandfather had given him when he was fifteen. He hadn't told her about setting the horse free, since that was both illegal and frowned upon, instead letting her think that Blue had escaped on his own and joined a band of mustangs.

"And he's far away. It's a long ride." Kade slapped half a dozen small pancakes onto a red plastic plate, handed it to his daughter, then started pouring more batter into the frying pan.

"I can make it," Maddie said as she covered her pancakes with syrup.

"Maybe you can, but can Sugar Foot? You're getting pretty big and riding double might be kind of hard on the old girl."

"Da-ad."

Kade smiled in response to her disgusted tone. He hated what his long-ago mistake had done to Libby, but never for one instant had he regretted his child. And he was doing the best he could to be a decent father, even though he didn't have a lot of experience in that area. At least he'd hung around with his friend Menace's huge family and Jason Ross's smaller one enough to have some experiences of what a real family was supposed to be like.

"Maybe when I get my other horse we can ride out and see if we can find Blue."

"Cool. When are you getting your other horse?" Maddie asked, practically bouncing in her seat. They'd been over this before, but Kade patiently repeated himself.

"As soon as I sell this place."

"And then you're moving back up by us, right?"

"Yeah." *I hope.* It was also possible he'd

have to go wherever he could find a decent job or—and he'd just started playing with this idea—where he could go to school. Get some training.

"And then I can ride the new horse all the time. Whenever I ask Mike for a horse, he says we don't have room."

"He has a point there, kiddo. Not many horses like living in a small backyard."

"We can board him."

"That's expensive."

"Mike's rich."

Not really, though compared to Kade he was. Kade refrained from commenting.

"Maybe when you move back, I can keep my horse with you?" Maddie held out her plate for seconds, having inhaled the first batch of pancakes.

"It may be a while before I get my own place."

"I thought *you'd* be rich when you sell the house. You know, like you used to be."

Or had thought he was.

"I wish," Kade said. But if all went well, he should have enough to invest in a smaller property and pay for some kind of training. It just might not be in the immediate Elko area. "But no matter what, I'll be close enough that we'll get our time together, right?"

Kade's cell phone rang just as he sent Maddie off to shower. She lingered at the door, shamelessly eavesdropping.

"This is Joe Barton of the Zephyr Valley ranch," the man on the phone said without bothering to include a hello. "We met at the feed store."

"I remember."

"I apologize for being brusque then, but…"

"I understand," Kade said. "Zero tends to be enthusiastic."

"Yes. Exactly. And I didn't know you from Adam. Didn't connect the name until later. Anyway, would you be interested in riding some colts for me? I have three that need some miles."

"I'm waiting to hear on a job." Or three. "I'm not sure how much time I'll have if it pans out."

"I'm flexible. I'm sure we can work something out."

"Zephyr Valley—" it almost hurt Kade to call the old Boggy Flat by that name "—is quite a drive from here. I'd want to have the colts here at my ranch while I'm riding them."

"What are your facilities like? I don't keep my horses in barbed wire."

"Then I guess you won't be keeping them here, unless they all stay in the one corral and you provide hay. My pastures have wire fences."

"Do you mind if I stop by and see where you'd keep 'em? Maybe iron out some details?"

"Sure. I'll be home all day."

"What do you charge a month?"

"A grand per animal," Kade said without hesitation. He had a feeling Joe Barton wanted to tell people that world champion cowboy Kade Danning had finished his colts. And he'd discovered over the years that some people didn't feel as if they were getting quality anything unless they paid through the nose.

"Nine hundred, if I provide the hay."

"Agreed."

"Who was that, Dad?" Maddie asked from the bathroom doorway.

"A guy who wants me to ride some colts for him." And a nice surprise bit of income.

Maddie's eyes widened. "Then I get Sugar Foot all to myself next time I visit."

Kade smiled. "If he brings colts, you can ride Sugar Foot."

"I wish Sugar Foot was all coal black with a white star. That's what my next horse is going to be. Or maybe a blue roan." She swung the door back and forth as she talked, then suddenly she stopped moving. "Hey. When you get the colts, then we can go see Blue with the wild horses." Her eyes got even rounder as the idea began to gel. "We can camp out! And put ropes around our sleeping bags to keep snakes away and hobble the horses, like in my Phantom Stallion book."

Kade fell back on one of those parental phrases he found he used over and over again. "We'll see."

"It'll be so much fun."

As much fun as horse camp? Somehow he thought not. A trip to the mustangs would be one or maybe two days at the most. Horse camp was three weeks. Hard to compare the two.

He couldn't wait until he had this place sold and he could move closer to Maddie—

close enough to fight for the time that was legally his.

Libby would probably organize a parade to celebrate his departure.

CHAPTER THREE

JILLIAN AND MIKE PULLED into Kade's yard around four that afternoon. Mike was an accountant for one of the big mines in Elko. Quiet and unassuming. Kade had to admit that Mike was better for Jillian than he had ever been, but when Maddie ran and gave him a big hug Kade found it a little hard to take. She really did have two dads, and Kade sometimes had a sneaking suspicion that he wasn't number one.

But he wasn't giving up. Maybe he had some stuff to make up for, but for the most part he'd been there for his daughter—and he would continue to be there.

Jillian eyed the house, with its peeling paint and dirty windows, while Mike loaded Maddie's purple suitcase in the trunk of the car. Her expression was pained.

"We stayed in the trailer," Kade said.

"Good. I don't want her exposed to hanta-virus."

Like he would let his kid be anywhere near mice. "Give me some credit, all right?"

Jillian sniffed. "When Maddie comes back here in June, will she be staying in the trailer? Or will the house be ready for habitation?" She smoothed her wind-ruffled hair away from her face as she spoke. It was a lighter brown than it had been when they'd been married. And streaked in a classy kind of way.

"I plan on having the house done by the time she gets here. If not, well, we've stayed in the trailer before."

"But not for weeks, Kade. And when are you going to tell her she won't be going to horse camp?"

"I'm not, Jillian. You're the one who set that up—you explain it to her." Kade was in a lose-lose situation, thanks to his ex-wife, and when they'd finally discussed the matter over the phone she hadn't been one bit repentant.

"I get Maddie for two months every summer. It's part of the agreement," Kade continued.

"It's not in her best interest. I thought you would understand that. Whatever happened between us, you always put Maddie's well-being first."

That's it, Jillie. Slap down the guilt card.

"I allowed you to reduce child support," she said with a tilt of her head.

"That was temporary. And I made it up."

"But I cooperated."

"Jillian, I want to see my daughter for the summer, as per the agreement. I don't want to have to get a lawyer."

He couldn't afford a lawyer, and unfortunately, due to his having to temporarily lower his child-support payments while he'd fought his way out of the financial bind his crooked ex-accountant had left him in, she knew that.

"Do what's best for Maddie, Kade. I'll give you a couple days to think about it and then we'll talk again. Oh…you really don't need to send the support checks this summer, if it's a burden."

"Are you trying to buy me off?"

"I'm trying to do what's best for my daughter."

"*Our* daughter."

"Do you have a means of support?"

"I'm doing all right." Kind of.

"Well, if you're working, then who'll take care of Maddie?"

"Damn it, Jill…"

She started walking. "I'll call in a few days, Kade, and we can discuss this some more."

She got into the car, where Mike was waiting behind the wheel and Maddie was arranging her nest of blankets and pillows in the backseat beside the twins, leaving Kade seething. He faked a smile and raised a hand to wave to Maddie as they drove away. Mike waved back, too. Jillian didn't.

Okay, maybe he wouldn't go to work until after Maddie left. That was the way things would probably pan out, anyway, since he'd checked with every place he'd sent an application to and there were no bites so far. But on the bright side, riding colts for Joe Barton would help immensely, plus it was something he could do while Maddie was there and he'd still have time left to work on the house. Besides that, Maddie would only be there for a matter of a few weeks, unless he got tough with Jillian. But what kind of father kept his daughter from going to horse camp? Even he wasn't delusional enough to imagine that riding with Dad would be as much fun as spending three weeks with other girls and lots of horses. There'd probably be campfires and marshmallows and girl talk.

Was Maddie old enough for girl talk?

It kind of tore at him to think that even if she wasn't now, she soon would be. Kids grew up fast—faster than he'd ever dreamed. So why had his childhood seemed to last forever?

Must have been the fear factor.

Kade stared at the evil house in which he'd planned to spend the day, then turned his back on it and walked to his truck. The house would keep. Right now he was going to attend to some other unfinished business. Libby might not want to hear what he had to say, but he needed to say it.

LIBBY HAD JUST finished filling her horses' water troughs when she heard a vehicle pull into her yard. Buster and Jiggs, her Australian shepherds, shot around the side of the barn at the sound of tires on gravel.

Libby wiped her damp hands down the sides of her jeans and followed the dogs, hoping she was about to come face-to-face with a traveling salesman—anyone other than Kade.

No such luck. Kade was crouched next to his truck, petting her traitorous dogs, who were taking turns licking his face.

"To the porch," Libby ordered. The Aussies slowly obeyed, slinking away from Kade and casting Libby dark canine glances as they headed for the house.

Kade stood up. A good ten feet separated them. It didn't feel like enough space. "You fixed the place up nice," he said.

And she had, pouring all the work into it that her parents never had, due to their addictions. The barn had a proper roof now, and the pastures were well fenced. Her small house wasn't the greatest, but she'd planted flowers all around it and someday she'd redo the inside. Someday.

"Yeah. Thanks." Libby shoved her hands into the back pockets of her worn jeans. One of her fingers poked out of a hole that had worn through because of her fencing pliers. "Why are you here?"

"There're still some things I want to straighten out."

Libby shook her head. "I believe that everything between us is as straight as it's going to get."

"I beg to differ."

"Differ all you want. And while you're differing, maybe you could get into your truck and drive away."

He advanced a couple slow steps forward. Libby held her ground, which wasn't easy since every nerve in her body seemed to be screaming at her to back up.

"You came to see *me*," he said in a reasonable tone once he'd come to a halt.

She pulled her hands out of her pockets, crossed them over her chest. "I came to tell you that I didn't want you stirring up gossip."

"Bull. You've never been concerned about gossip in your life."

He had her there.

"All right. I'll admit it—I wanted to get the damned reunion over with, since we were bound to run into each other sometime. I didn't want an audience when it happened. Okay? I didn't come to make friends with you."

"Libby, a lot of stuff has happened since—" He gestured with one hand, but Libby cut him off before he could start talking again.

"I don't want to hear about it." She kicked a pebble with her foot, watched it bounce a couple times and then looked up at him, determined to get things straight once and for all, if that was truly what he wanted. Then maybe he'd leave.

"Here's the deal, Kade. I *trusted* you. You were my lover and I trusted you." She stopped, surprised that the corners of her mouth had started to quiver. It only took a second to regain control, but Kade had noticed. "I never thought you'd let me down."

"There were circumstances."

"Circumstances?" She couldn't believe the force of anger that surged through her. "Circumstances? What circumstances led you to screw another woman—and knock her up?"

"*Stop.*"

He meant it. His face had turned pale. Libby shoved both hands through her curls, tilting her chin and squeezing her eyes shut, trying to get a grip. He probably didn't want to think of his daughter as the result of knocking someone up. Even if it was true.

She opened her eyes but didn't look at him. Instead, she focused momentarily on the gravel at her feet.

"Kade, I can tell you right now we're not going to talk this through. We're not going to shake hands and let bygones be bygones. I can't do it." She finally met his gaze. "I don't even want to try."

And then she turned and headed for the house, reinforcing her words with action, hoping Kade had the good sense to get in that truck and drive away. If he didn't, things might get ugly.

Fortunately Kade knew trouble when he saw it. She heard the truck door open and shut, then the engine chug to life.

Libby kept walking.

AS SOON AS HE got home, Kade backed up to his dad's old stock trailer. A few minutes later the trailer was hitched and he was out in the pasture slipping a halter on his horse.

A couple of hours in the mountains and then he'd go to work on the house, when he wasn't so frustrated and pissed off that he could barely see straight. He'd had it in his mind to do two things when he moved back to Otto—make peace with Libby, or at least attempt to make peace, and find Blue. Obviously he wouldn't be making peace with Lib, but maybe he could find his old horse and see if he'd managed to do one thing in life that hadn't later turned to crap.

Kade parked the trailer and unloaded his horse in almost the same spot where he and Libby had parked their "borrowed" horse trailer fourteen years ago. There was a very real possibility that something had happened to Blue since they'd released him, but Kade was hoping that wasn't the case. He wanted to see the stud running free, with many red and blue roan foals at the sides of his mares.

He smiled at the image, the tension in his muscles easing as he recalled the exhilaration, the sense of empowerment he'd felt when he'd turned Blue loose, slapping him on the butt and sending him off the hill to join the mustang herd.

Take that, Dad.

He and Libby had known enough about herd dynamics to realize Blue wouldn't be welcome, but would hang about on the periphery until he'd managed to steal a few mares of his own. They'd discussed the possibility that Blue might not survive, but to Kade, young as he was, he thought it would be better for Blue to die in the wild than to be abused by an angry man. Kade's father.

So they'd borrowed a trailer from Menace's dad, taking it late at night without permission, and then they'd led Blue through the pasture and out the far gate to load him in the trailer on the county road so there'd be no suspicious tracks. A two-hour drive over to the Manning Valley, with Libby sitting close to him. They'd arrived at dawn, released Blue and been back in town by six o'clock. Menace's trailer was back behind the barn and Libby had her dad's truck in the garage before he'd come home from the bar. Kade had climbed in through his bedroom window and sprawled across his bed. Fifteen minutes later his dad had slammed the door open and told him to get his sorry carcass out of bed and go feed. Which Kade had done, coming back in a few minutes later to tell his dad that the blue stud was gone.

Kade had spent the rest of that day hovering between the satisfaction of knowing that the stud was safe and out-and-out fear. He'd been unable to meet up with Libby for several days, due to his old man's fury. His dad hadn't let him out of his sight.

Now Kade mounted and started up a road that would soon deteriorate into a rocky trail. A mustang trail. He sucked in a deep breath of mountain air. It had been too long since he'd been out here. He and Maddie had ridden around his rented property in Boise before he'd sold his second horse, but other than that, he hadn't spent enough time in the saddle. He'd be rectifying that.

When he topped the pass leading into the next valley, he paused to let his horse have a breather. The meadow below was greening up, but the junipers and brush around it were little more than twisted black snags—evidence of a fire. The creek still ran through the meadow, pooling up at one end, but he could see that this was no longer the mustangs' watering hole. In fact, he hadn't seen a single sign of the herd.

He made a slight movement with his rein hand and his mount started to pick her way down the rocky trail to the meadow. If the mustangs weren't watering there, where were they?

He drew his horse up and reversed course. He'd ride the ridge line and check the next drainage. They had to be somewhere close. Mustangs kept to their own range.

Six hours later he dismounted at the trailer. Both he and his horse were exhausted and he was by now certain that the mustang herd no longer resided in this valley.

Had some natural disaster wiped them out? There were fire scars. Disease? Had someone shot them?

Libby was a wild horse specialist. She would know.

And she'd be *so* happy to see him.

Maybe he'd wait a day or two before he asked.

ALMOST A WEEK had passed and Libby was still stewing over Kade's recent visit. And it didn't help that she couldn't stop forming a mental picture of Kade and his daughter whenever she looked across the field and saw the lights of his trailer. The girl holding on to his belt, Kade putting a protective hand on her thin shoulder. Those little silver hearts and hot-pink kitties on the pjs.

Kade was a dad. He knew about parenting and diapers and midnight feedings. He'd experienced things that Libby was beginning to think she never would experience. Sure, she dated. She liked men. But every time someone got close, she felt the need to send him packing. Togetherness made her freeze. As a consequence, she generally didn't didn't date guys who wanted to put down roots.

She wasn't certain if her commitment phobia was a character flaw or the result of Kade screwing around on her. Or if it went back even further than that, back to the time she'd finally figured out that not all parents were so busy drinking that they didn't have time for their kid.

But she'd made her own family ties by then, attaching herself to Jason's and Menace's families, as had Kade. Since she and Kade had the most in common, however, and lived closest to one another, they'd hung together the most, understood each other the best—which was exactly why she'd never comprehended what had happened between them. She'd decided long ago that she wasn't going to waste any more of her life trying to figure it out. The past was just that, and she was moving forward—if she could just get that damned father-daughter snapshot out of her head and stop feeling the jabs of pain that came with it.

Libby finally gave up and closed the

computer file she'd been working on. She wasn't accomplishing anything while her thoughts were all over the place, and she needed to concentrate as she tabulated the research results of a two-year range study. Then, as soon as she was done with the tabulations, she would write her section of a report that weighed the effects of animal usage, including cattle, native herds of deer, antelope and elk and mustangs. Which animals had the most impact on the land, which needed to be cut back during certain negative conditions. And most importantly, the optimum numbers that the range could sustain.

Glen, her former boss, had started the project the year before he retired, and she, Stephen and Fred, her coworkers, had spent the past eighteen months gathering data, as well as searching archived reports for information. Now, with no end to the drought in sight, the findings would be used as the basis for making some serious land-usage decisions. Libby wanted to be as careful and accurate as possible with her part of the report—which meant that this was not the time to work on it.

She reached for the phone and dialed the

number for Menace's service station. "This has been one long week," she said as soon he answered.

"You at work or home?"

"Home." Such as it was. Libby glanced around her living room, thinking she really had to spend less time in the barn and more time making her house a home. But right now her animals were more important to her than new curtains or furniture.

"Lucky you," Menace grumbled.

"I did four ten-hour days this week," she retorted. And thanks to Ellen and a series of "important" yet useless meetings, it felt as if she'd worked six ten-hour days. "So…are we on for this evening?"

"What do you mean, are we on?" Menace asked, sounding shocked. "It's chorizo night at the bar. Of course we're on."

Chorizo night. Great. Libby wasn't really a fan, but the Basque sausages were a local favorite, and she'd much rather lose herself in a crowd than sit at home and brood about what was. And wasn't.

"I only asked because I heard you've made a new friend and I thought you might have other plans," she said.

Menace coughed. "Uh, what new friend?"

"Your new female friend." The one the waitresses at the café had been buzzing about when Libby had stopped to pick up dinner on her way home the night before. The new owner of the hardware store. Ginger someone.

"No plans," he said stiffly.

"I'd like to meet her."

"I'm taking it slow. Don't want to scare her off, you know?"

"Good idea." And it was about time. Menace had dreadful luck with women, and part of the problem was that his enthusiasm at actually being *with* a woman often overwhelmed the new girlfriend. "See you around eight?"

"Sure. But what if, you know, Kade shows up, too?"

"We already cleared the air." Sort of. Enough for him to stay away from her, she hoped.

"Any broken bones?" Menace was only half joking.

"No," Libby said with a sigh. If only it had been that simple.

"Glad to hear it," Menace said. "You can't go living your life being mad at someone."

"I never said I wasn't mad," Libby said softly. "See you tonight." She hung up and went to the back porch, where she slipped into her barn boots, whistled for the dogs and went out to feed her horses. Four hours to burn. Four hours to think too much. Maybe it was a good time to muck out the stalls.

JOE BARTON SHOWED up with three beautiful colts late Friday afternoon, colts that radiated breeding and money. Joe had come to inspect the premises before allowing his animals to stay with Kade, but since Kade had put in two backbreaking days bringing the corrals up to standard, fixing the sagging gates and rebuilding the mangers and wind shelters, Joe had no problem with what Kade had to offer. He'd stayed while Kade started ground work with the first colt, a black Appaloosa with a splashy blanket.

"I can see this will work out just fine," Joe said when Kade released the colt and caught the second. "I'd heard good things." He smoothed his mustache with a forefinger. "You know, I was in the stands the night that bronc beat the snot out of you. I apologize for not recognizing you at the feed store."

"Not one of my better nights," Kade said, tying the colt to the hitching rail. "And I don't really want to be remembered for being beat up."

"You came back."

"I did." He just hoped he could do it again, prove he wasn't a loser.

"You don't mind if I stop by to check progress?"

"Anytime you want," Kade said. "I, uh, want half the payment now. The other half when the thirty days are up."

Barton reached for his wallet and damned if he didn't give him cash. "I want a receipt."

"Sure." It would have been cool to whip out a regular receipt book, but instead, Kade went into the horse trailer and wrote a receipt on the legal pad he used for his grocery lists. He handed the yellow paper to Barton, who took it and folded it carefully into quarters.

"If you don't mind my asking, what happened to you?" Barton asked as he put the receipt in his shirt pocket.

Kade tucked his hands into his back pockets. "You mean why aren't I living the high life?" *Why am I wearing boots that need to be resoled while you're wearing brand-new eelskin?*

"Pretty much."

"Just the way things worked out, Mr. Barton." He wasn't going to recite a litany of his life errors for this guy.

Barton patted the colt that Kade had just haltered. "If I'm happy with these, there'll be more."

"You'll be happy," Kade said. Because if there was one thing Kade understood, it was horses.

"I hope so. I have some friends who wouldn't mind having a world champion cowboy tune up their horses."

Kade just smiled. The irony was that riding broncs and starting colts had about as much in common as did competing in a demolition derby and teaching drivers' ed. Both might involve cars, but there weren't a whole lot of similarities beyond that. If Barton wanted to pay for Kade's name, however, Kade wouldn't dissuade him. He'd do an excellent job on the colts, get paid well and they'd both be happy.

Joe left after Kade had worked the third colt, a skittish chestnut that was more difficult to handle than the other two. Kade put away his tack, then went to sit in his lawn chair and stare at the house as if it was an adversary. Which, in a sense, it was.

He wasn't going in there tonight. He'd spent enough time alone, working on it. He felt antsy. Edgy. After he'd stopped drinking, he'd also stopped socializing for the most part. It was the surest way to avoid temptation, so he'd spent a lot of time alone. Alone was nothing new.

Maybe that was the problem.

CHAPTER FOUR

THE CUPBOARDS WERE almost bare and the propane was getting low in the tanks.

Kade realized he was searching for an excuse to go to town, so why not just go? And while there, maybe he'd stop by the café and grab a bite. He'd avoided public places in Otto because he hated playing Kade Danning, rodeo champion, when that was no longer who he was. And it bothered him that people who'd ignored him back when he'd been just ordinary Kade Danning, a local kid who could have used some support while dealing with his asshole dad, now embraced him. But if he was going to be here for months and months, which seemed a definite possibility considering the condition of his father's property, then he needed to reintroduce himself to Otto society, such as it was.

As he drove past the bar he noticed there

were more vehicles than was normal for eight o'clock, but the hand-lettered Chorizo Night sign explained the full lot.

Libby's truck was parked next to the building, and yet he pulled in anyway, citing the adage about it being a free country. He no longer drank, but what better night than Chorizo Night to say hello to his neighbors?

He spotted Libby immediately sitting at a table with Dennis Mann—Menace, they'd all called him back in high school. A tall, fair-haired guy carrying a plate filled with beans and salad, chorizo in a bun balanced on top, sat down next to Libby and she smiled at him. A few minutes later Jason Ross and a pretty blonde sat down. He'd heard Jason had gotten married. That had to be the new missus.

Kade automatically started searching for a place to sit on the other side of the room, prior to getting in line. Someone said his name and he turned to see Cal Johnson, one of his old classmates, now wearing a deputy sheriff's uniform and sporting a shaved head.

"I've been planning to stop by and say hello," Cal said. "You saved me the trouble."

"Glad to oblige," Kade said, shaking his hand.

More people gathered around and before

long he was in the center of a crowd at the end of the food line, renewing old acquaintances, some of which he wasn't even aware he'd had. A redhead who introduced herself as Trista attached herself to him, and it became clear that he was no longer destined to be lonely if he didn't choose to be. He was starting to feel just a bit claustrophobic. And also like a fraud. It'd been three years since he'd won a buckle, and during one of those years he'd actively tried to destroy himself. He wasn't really hometown-hero material. But the novelty of having a two-bit celebrity around would wear off eventually, and then maybe he could actually hang with some people. Be just plain Kade Danning.

He pulled out his wallet, paid the cashier ten bucks, got a paper plate in return and started loading up. Cal waved him over to his small table and squeezed in chairs for both Kade and Trista, who'd followed.

"I just love a good chorizo," she said with a half smile. No doubting her meaning. Kade smiled noncommittally, then glanced in Libby's direction. The blond guy had said something, and she was laughing. Kade took too big a bite of his chorizo and almost choked.

Maybe he should have stayed home.

"KADE'S HERE." Jason sat down with his plate of food.

"I know," Libby replied. She'd spotted him almost as soon as he entered the building, as if her Kade radar had been on. It had been just a matter of time until they ended up in the same place at the same time, Otto being as small as it was. She was glad now that she'd gone to see him and that they'd gotten the first big meet-up out of the way. It made things easier. Not great by any means, but easier.

Which made her wonder, did all people feel this much pain over ex-lovers years later? She didn't have a lot of experience in that particular arena, since she never allowed herself to get serious about anyone. It saved a lot of wear and tear on her emotions.

"Who's Kade?" Kira, Jason's wife, asked.

"A blast from the past." Libby lifted her glass to her lips. No doubt Jason would explain all to his wife later.

Less than an hour after he'd arrived, Kade got to his feet, said his goodbyes to Cal

Johnson and the other people at his table and headed for the rear exit. Libby was not at all surprised to see Trista, who'd been cozied up to him since he'd arrived, follow him out the door.

She was, however, surprised to see Trista come back in a few minutes later, her expression bordering on angry. Perhaps Kade had learned to say no, after all. Too bad it was a few years too late.

The jukebox started up, overly loud as always, and Libby accepted a challenge from Menace to play a game of pool. Life went on, and it didn't really matter if Kade was in Otto or not.

Later, while Kira and Libby's vet and occasional escort, Stan, were playing one of the worst games of pool Libby had ever witnessed, Jason came to stand next to her. Together they leaned back against the wall, watching the action and occasionally wincing as an easy shot went askew.

"Doing all right?" Jason finally asked in a gruff, man-not-comfortable-talking-about-emotions voice.

"I haven't been hit by the cue ball yet."

"That wasn't what I meant."

"I'm doing fine in every possible way." She shifted her gaze sideways toward Jason. "I went to see him." She didn't have to explain which him she meant.

"Yeah?"

She moistened her lips. "I met his daughter. Cute kid."

Jason didn't reply. At least *one* of them wasn't playing a game.

"I'm still angry," she said in a low voice, giving up the act as she brought her attention back to the pool table. "I don't want to feel a damned thing. Nothing. But I can't help it. It's disturbing." On many levels. She exhaled and went silent for a moment before saying philosophically, "He'll be gone as soon as the ranch sells."

"Have you seen what kind of shape that ranch is in? It'll be a while before he gets it ready."

She gave Jason a sharp look. "Any more good news?"

"I don't think he'll bother you." Jason smiled a little as Libby's eyes narrowed suspiciously. "Couldn't help myself."

"Jason, keep your nose out of my business. It's kind of embarrassing to have a self-appointed big brother taking care of business that I need to handle myself."

But Libby would have done the same for him in a similar situation. In fact, she'd once made an attempt to protect him from the woman who eventually became his wife. Considering the circumstances, though, she'd been justified.

"I understa— *Whoa!*" Jason jerked sideways, bumping into her, as a ball flew off the table, barely missing him before bouncing off the wall.

"Sorry," Stan muttered. He took the ball from Jason, put it back on the table and started lining up his next shot.

LIBBY WAS IN A mood the next day, but fortunately no one came close enough to achieve injured-bystander status. Actually all of the employees of the Wesley BLM field office were maintaining low profiles, and whenever Ellen did a walkabout the staff made an effort to appear busy, even if she'd just cut funding for their current project in her massive rear-rangement of the budget and now they had little to do.

Ellen seemed quite happy, though. She'd

patrol the offices at least twice a day, her perfectly polished glasses sparkling in the dim fluorescent light. Ellen was forever polishing something—her glasses, her desk, her résumé.

Everyone on staff had taken a hit that week except for Libby, who still was working on her recommendations for the range-usage report. Not much Ellen could do about that, since it was almost completed, but Libby's office mate Stephen had lost his project. He was now busy planning a totally unnecessary range survey in order to justify his existence. Being the newest person on the staff, he was one of Ellen's favorite victims, and now he sat with his head down, his lanky body hunched over his desk, his wire-rimmed glasses sliding down his nose as he concentrated and tried to make himself invisible.

Several other people had suffered similar hits. The Wesley office was becoming a bureaucratic nightmare. Ellen's work here was almost done. And no one would write a negative word on her supervisory evaluation because they all wanted the woman promoted and gone.

"Libby…"

Libby grimaced at the sound of Ellen's voice, set her pencil down on her desk with extreme care and rose to her feet. She straightened her shirt, then followed Ellen down the hall to Ellen's office. Her boss indicated a map laid out on the desk.

"I've noticed that you seem to be concentrating your herd-management efforts on these two areas." She pointed. "Why is that?"

"One herd was affected by the recent range fires and the other is the one where we're studying the effects of the contraceptive program."

"I'm not so much interested in herds as in *areas*," Ellen said.

Areas? "I don't follow you."

"The area that needs the most management is here." Again Ellen pointed at a location on the map, making Libby wonder if they were speaking the same language.

"That herd is in fine shape. Not too big, not too small. The range is holding up well." Which was why they had relocated the mustangs to that particular region after a devastating fire two years ago. It had turned out to be a wise decision.

"There's some question about that."

Libby raised her eyebrows. This was the first she'd heard of a problem with that range. She was about to say so when Ellen clipped out, "Those are all the questions I have. For now."

"Fine." Libby headed for the door. *She* had questions now, but she wasn't going to ask them of Ellen. She would gather more information and find out what her boss was getting at first.

KADE HAD KNOWN better than to use his dad's ancient Chevy truck when he made a dump run Friday afternoon, but it carried more trash than his own short-bed truck and he'd felt like driving the old beast again. Besides which, it needed the carbon blown out of the engine, and he was in a mood to do just that.

Unfortunately, on the way back from the dump, he blew more than carbon. If he wasn't mistaken, he'd just blown a rod.

Kade got out of the truck and lifted the heavy hood, propping it open as heat rolled off the engine. Crap. Now he had a walk ahead of him, because his phone was in the pocket of the jeans he'd changed out of prior to loading the trash. Even if he'd had his phone, however, who would he have called? He didn't have anyone's number—except for Libby's landline, which he still knew by heart. Wouldn't be calling Libby, that was for sure.

A rooster tail of dust appeared down the road where it hooked onto the paved state highway, and Kade felt a small surge of hope. Maybe he could catch a ride, take advantage of his status as a washed-up minor celebrity.

As the vehicle neared, though, he realized he'd have no such luck. It was Jason Ross.

After their exchange in the hardware store Kade fully expected Jason to drive on by, but instead he pulled to a stop on the opposite side of the road and rolled down his window.

"You appear to have a situation," he said in a flat voice.

"What's new?" Kade asked, irritated. He didn't need people stopping by and pointing out the obvious. He was about to say words to that effect when Jason asked, "You want a lift?"

The words came out grudgingly, but Kade figured this was no time to resent the less-than-enthusiastic delivery of an invitation. Not unless he wanted to walk four miles in old cowboy boots. "I'd appreciate it."

"Hop in."

Kade got into the passenger side of Jason's truck, something he'd done a couple of thousand times during high school. His old man had rarely let him drive the very truck he was now leaving by the side of the road, but Jason had always had wheels and been happy to share. Back then Libby was usually sitting between them wherever they went, whether it was to a party, on a hunting trip or to a rodeo. Probably a good thing she wasn't there now, Kade reflected, since it would put the odds at two against one. When push came to shove, Jason would side with Lib.

"Are you going to call Menace?" Jason asked.

"I don't think I'll have it fixed. I may just tow it home, then sell it as is with the ranch." Which brought another thought to mind. He cast Jason a sideways glance. "Cal Johnson told me your wife's family is in ranch and farm real estate."

Jason nodded without taking his eyes off the road. "Yeah, they are."

"Would it be worth my while to call them? About my place, I mean." Kade was probably pushing things, but he felt certain Jason would set him straight if he was. "I had Marvin look it over, but…he doesn't exactly inspire confidence."

Jason actually smiled. "Well, Marvin's only had his shingle out for a few months now, and I don't think he's made too many sales."

"So what about your in-laws?"

"They pretty much stick to big-money deals. And if they did buy your ranch, they'd probably chop it into lots. It's the way they do business."

Kade shrugged. "If they can sell the lots, more power to them. I don't care what happens to the ranch once I'm gone." No truer words had ever been spoken. Kade couldn't wait to unload the place, along with the memories, to move on, start over.

"Maybe your neighbors care."

"I'm not trying to screw my neighbors, but I've got to sell and I've got to get as much out of it as I can. I had some trouble with the IRS."

"I heard." Jason turned the corner into Kade's driveway, then pulled to a stop next to the barn. He shifted in his seat to face Kade. "You, uh, might talk to Kira. My wife.

She and her sister have their own real-estate business. Kira handles small ranch sales in Nevada and her sister takes care of those up in Idaho."

"After talking to you in the hardware store, I didn't think you wanted me hanging around your womenfolk."

"Yeah." There was a touch of chagrin in Jason's expression. "I've been thinking. What happens between you and Libby isn't any of my business. It's just that…well, I don't want to see her—" he hesitated "—like she was."

"For that to happen, she'd probably have to stop hating me, and I don't see that on the horizon."

"Good point."

"Yeah," Kade said, because he couldn't think of anything else to say. "So, do you think your wife could stop by and take a look at the ranch and give me some advice on how to make it most salable?"

"I'll have her call you. There's a pen in the console. Write your number on something."

Kade wrote his cell number on the back of a receipt. "Thanks," he said as he handed the paper to Jason.

"No problem."

And it sounded as if he might actually mean it.

KADE HAD JUST entered the trailer when his cell phone rang. Maddie's name appeared on the screen and he picked up immediately. School was barely out—Maddie never called this early, before her homework was done.

"Dad, Mom says that if I visit you, I can't go to horse camp!" She sounded both angry and distressed.

Thanks, Jillian. "Honey—"

"Shandy gets to go, Dad, and we wanted to share a bunk bed and everything."

"Maddie, we'll work something out." Riding horses with Dad wasn't going to compete with riding horses and sharing a bunk bed with her best friend. "Could I talk to your mom?"

Maddie instantly yelled for Jillian, holding the phone close enough so that Kade winced at the volume.

"Well, I'm the bad guy," he said as soon as his ex said hello, "which isn't fair, Jill, because all I want is what I'm supposed to get according to our agreement. Thanks a lot."

"I thought that you of all people would want Maddie to have this experience," Jillian said primly.

"I want my time with my daughter."

"Then why did you move to Otto?"

"You know why."

Jillian's voice dropped as she said, "Yes. And if you remember I warned you about Dylan Smith. I told you I thought something about him was off. But no. You said he was a friend and doing a great job handling your money."

"Damn it, this isn't about my accountant or my stupidity or anything else. I paid for that mistake." *And several others.* "I'm fixing it the quickest way I can. And meanwhile, I want to see my kid."

"Fine. I'll tell her."

Thus making him the bad guy. She'd set him up well on this one. Maddie would come for the summer. And she might even have some fun. But she'd be thinking about what she was missing, and Shandy would have stories to tell. Oh, yeah. Kade couldn't win here.

"Don't. But we *will* work something out. If not, I honestly am seeing a lawyer."

"Don't threaten me, Kade."

"Then follow the agreement. What you did

this time… We agreed not to play Maddie as a pawn against each other."

"I'm not doing that! I'm just trying to keep her life stable."

"By shutting me out?" Kade asked quietly.

There was a long silence.

"I'm her dad, Jill. Her real dad. She has a right to know me and I have a right to know her. And I'm serious about the lawyer."

"I believe you."

"Let me talk to Maddie."

Kade told Maddie she'd be going to horse camp and that she could spend a couple of weeks with him in June and August—which was about all the time she had after school ended and before it started again. Not the best solution, but one that would work. For Maddie, anyway.

By the time Kade hung up, his daughter was happy again, and he was wavering between feeling good that he'd made everything all right with her, and depressed because he'd really wanted them to spend more time together during the summer.

LIBBY GOT HOME from work mentally spent. It was exhausting to hold both her tongue and her temper for ten hours. That woman had to go.

After finishing with Libby, Ellen had browbeaten both Stephen and Fred. Fred didn't care, but Stephen had come back to the office looking like a whipped pup. The only positive note was that they were about to have a four-day break from the Ellen regime while she attended a state conference.

"I tell you," Fred had grumbled, rubbing a hand over the gray bristles on top of his head, "one of us needs to go along and keep a rein on her. Who knows what kind of lies she'll tell or what she'll promise to do?"

But Ellen wasn't allowing anyone to go— probably for the same reasons that Fred had suggested.

The more Libby thought about it, the more certain it seemed that Ellen was up to something—and it probably involved accumulating political support. Ellen didn't so much want to do a competent job as a *showy* job, one that would get her the promotion she wanted as she climbed government ranks. It ticked Libby off that in order to better her own position, Ellen would probably do things that were actually detrimental to the area but looked great on paper. And there wasn't much Libby could do about it. But what she could do, she would.

Libby drove up to her house and instantly knew something was wrong when the Aussies came shooting out of the pasture, instead of appearing from the porch. She parked and jumped out of the truck, running toward the pasture. There at the far end she could see that one of her horses was down. Colic? If so, she had to act fast. She felt in her pocket for her phone, then realized it was back in the truck. She didn't slow down.

It wasn't colic.

Her best gelding, Cooper, was on his back with his feet in the air, entangled in strands of smooth wire fencing, his sides heaving as he struggled to breathe. It looked as if he'd rolled into the fence while taking a dust bath, got his feet caught in the wire and then panicked. His eyes showed white as Libby approached. She quickly assessed the situation and then raced back to the house, the dogs at her heels. She needed wire cutters and she needed help.

The vet was on speed dial, but when she hit Stan's number the answering service came on, telling her he was away for the week and to contact his colleague, Sam Hyatt, in Wesley. Libby didn't have time to wait for Sam to drive down from Wesley.

She hit Jason's number. He answered immediately and she blurted out her story.

"Lib, I'm in Elko," he said when she paused to take a breath.

Libby cursed, squeezing her eyes shut against tears of frustration. "I'll call Menace." She couldn't think of anything else to do.

There was no sound on the other end of the line for a few tense seconds, then Jason said, "Call Kade. He's close and he knows horses."

Libby's eyes snapped open. "Are you kidding?"

"He can get there fast and he'll be way more help than anyone else near your place. Especially Menace."

"I don't have Kade's number."

"He just gave it to me. Hold on a sec." When Jason gave her the number, she hung up, repeating the digits over and over until she'd punched them into the keypad. Kade answered on the second ring.

"It's Libby," she said without hesitation. "I have a horse down. I need help."

"Should I bring anything?"

"Wire cutters. Big ones. I'll be at the far end of the field."

The phone went dead and Libby grabbed her vet kit and headed out to where Cooper was struggling. She started working on the tautly stretched wire, trying to cut it with the only cutters she had at hand, but they were too small for the job. She needed her fencing pliers, wherever they might be.

Cooper's breathing was ragged, but Libby couldn't get the wire loose, much less get him back onto his side so that he could breathe better. She was frantically hacking away when she heard Kade speak behind her.

"Let me."

Libby backed off, letting him crouch down to use his cutters. He did live nearby, but he must have driven ninety miles an hour to get there that fast.

"Watch it," he said as he squeezed the handles. After the first wire popped, zinging wildly, he cut the second. The horse heaved, making the ends of a third wire, which was still wrapped around his hind leg, bounce.

"Damn," Kade murmured as he saw how tightly it was wound, cutting the animal's flesh.

He snapped the last wire, then started unwrapping it as Libby held the horse's head steady.

"I did everything I could to make the pastures safe."

Her parents had never done a damned thing for the small ranch, except let it fall down around them. When Libby had returned to Otto after college, she'd bought the property from them so that they could move to Arizona and continue drinking themselves to death.

The house and barn had been in fairly decent shape, only needing new roofs, which had almost bankrupted her, but the outbuildings were shot and the pastures had lain fallow for years. The fence posts were rotten and barbed wire was strewn everywhere, cropping up out of the ground in unexpected places, where a fence had gone down and had then been overgrown.

Libby had spent most of her free time cleaning wire out of the pastures and refencing them before she turned out her horses to graze. She didn't want any of her animals injured, and now one of her horses was.

"If you have animals, accidents will

happen," Kade said without looking at her. He glanced up at what was left of the fence. "He must have got caught while rolling."

"That's what I thought." It felt so odd, being there with Kade, agreeing with him, as if there was no bad history between them.

"Do you still ride him?"

"I did."

"You'll ride him again."

Libby swallowed hard as she watched Kade work, stroking the horse's neck to reassure him that she was there and that they were helping. Kade was probably right, but now Cooper's hind legs were badly skinned and burned where the wire had cut and rubbed against them. Recovery was going to take time.

"Do you have a clean area where we can treat him?" Kade asked as he carefully unwound the last bit of wire from Cooper's leg. The other horses were standing a short distance away, edging closer, curious about what was happening to their compadre.

"There's a stall in the barn," Libby said. "I'll have to run the rest of the horses into the next field so they don't escape."

"Go do that."

Libby jogged across the pasture to the gate. The horses, sensing greener grass on the other side of the fence, followed her. Libby opened the gate to let them walk through. By the time she crossed the field again, Kade had Cooper on his feet.

The horse took a tentative step forward and then another. The three of them walked slowly to the barn, Kade on one side of Cooper and Libby on the other, her hand on the gelding's neck, talking to him in a soothing voice.

"His leg will probably swell like crazy," Kade said once they had him in the stall. Libby had spread clean straw and then found a big roll of gauze. Together they cleaned and wrapped the damaged areas on Cooper's hind legs, duct-taping the top and bottom of the bandages to keep them from slipping off.

Kade opened his own first-aid kit and took out a plastic tube of horse analgesic, phenylbutazone, which he shoved into the corner of the horse's mouth, pushing the plunger all the way down.

"Do you want me to leave it?" he asked, referring to the medication.

She shook her head. "I have bute, too."

As she walked with Kade to his truck afterward, she felt as if she were waking from a dream, one in which events and actions that had seemed so reasonable at the time became utterly bizarre upon waking. She would never have expected to end the day by having Kade rescue her horse—or by feeling grateful that he'd come to help.

"Do you want me stop by in the morning to check the bandage?" Kade asked as he set his vet kit on the seat of his truck.

"I can handle it." She shoved her hands into her back pockets and glanced at the barn. "Thank you for coming."

"I did it for the horse."

Libby wasn't sure if he'd intended the comment to comfort or sting. It did both.

CHAPTER FIVE

KADE KNEW THAT LIBBY wanted him to leave now that the emergency was over, knew that she hated owing him. Well, he'd give her a chance to even things out.

"I need a favor, Libby."

"What?" she asked cautiously.

"Have you ever seen Blue when you've been doing your BLM horse stuff?"

He could see relief in her eyes. "A couple of times."

He forgot himself and smiled. Blue was alive. "I went searching for the herd a few days ago. Couldn't find it."

"We relocated it after the fires two years ago."

That explained a lot.

"How'd he look? How was he doing?"

Libby pressed her lips together. "He was getting a little poor the last time I saw him."

Her expression softened then, the mask dropped, and for a moment she was the old Libby. His friend. His lover. "He *is* almost twenty, Kade. It's a rough life out there."

"I want to find him. See him."

"Why?"

He didn't know exactly. Maybe because the horse had been the one positive thing in his youth besides Libby. And he'd messed things up with Lib, so that only left Blue. "I just…need to see him."

She frowned, but didn't pursue the matter. "I'll show you on a topo."

"Come with me," Kade said without even knowing why. Maybe it was because of that brief moment of empathy.

Libby actually took a step back. Not a good sign. No more empathy. "I don't think so."

He tried a different tack. "It would screw with the odds makers." A bad attempt at humor.

"As far as I'm concerned, the odds makers can go screw themselves." She kicked the toe of her boot into the gravel, glanced at the barn again, then met his gaze. "I owe you tonight, Kade. And I'll be nice to you tonight.

I'll show you where the herd is on a topo map."

"Never mind," he said in a clipped tone. "You can show me later." As if there would be a later. He got into his truck, and after checking to make sure the dogs were close to Libby he shifted into Reverse.

When he glanced in the rearview mirror on the way down the driveway he saw Libby walking back to the barn. Alone. And he was driving home. Alone.

What a waste.

THE NEXT MORNING Menace pulled into Kade's place with the Chevy on the back of his tow rig. "Where do you want her?" he asked gruffly.

"Behind the barn." To rot.

"Jason said you may want to sell."

"Do you know anyone who may want to buy it?" Because Kade knew someone who could use the cash.

"Yeah. But I can't guarantee you'd get much."

"I'll think about it," Kade said, and then he got to the subject that had been on his mind all morning. "Hey… do you see much of Libby?"

"Yeah, I do." It almost sounded like a threat.

"One of her horses got hurt last night and I thought maybe you could stop by and see if she needs some help changing the bandage. Apparently the vet is out of town." And Kade didn't think he'd be all that welcome now that she wasn't desperate.

"You *know* how I am with horses," Menace said, alarmed. Kade did know. Terrified.

"Oh. I thought maybe after all these years…"

"I'll stop by and see if she needs a hand. If so I can dig up someone." The big man had gone a little pale.

"Do that," Kade said. "And if you can't find anyone, call me. It's dangerous doctoring horses alone."

"Right. I will." Menace got back in his towtruck and put it in gear. He unloaded the Chevy behind the barn. "You want to pay me now or drop your insurance information by?"

"I'll pay you now." While he could. He pulled out his wallet.

"Check on Libby," he said as he handed over some of Joe Barton's cash. Menace nodded and got into his truck.

"WHAT THE HELL do you mean, Kade told you to check on me?"

Menace glared, his black beard making him look fierce. "I mean what I said. Kade thinks it's dangerous to take care of the horse by yourself and he's damned well right."

"Well, maybe he is, but I don't have to like it." Libby pulled her curls back in a rubber band, then grabbed her gloves off the kitchen table. "Come on, then. Let's go take care of business." She was aware that watching her doctor a horse was the last thing Menace wanted to do, but when she'd made a call to the vet in Wesley earlier that morning, he'd told her he had another client in Otto and it would be late afternoon before he could get there.

"Maybe we could call Benny Benson...." Menace ventured.

"Maybe you can just watch while I change the bandage. If the horse knocks me around, you can pick me up."

Menace's body stiffened. "If Kade's so worried about you, maybe he should have come over himself."

"He's welcome to do so," Libby lied as

she led the way to the pen, "but apparently he doesn't want to."

"Gee, I wonder why," Menace muttered.

Libby turned, took a long look at her big friend and then let out a sigh. "Sorry. Kade did me a favor last night. I hated asking and I don't like feeling beholden. Things are kind of…weird between us," she finished. Which was an understatement.

"Libby," Menace said, "if you're gonna live in the same community as him, you're gonna have to suck it up."

"I'm trying," she said as she opened the barn door. *But it isn't that easy.* She'd just rolled the door back when a truck pulled into the drive. Libby smiled. "Look, Menace…the cavalry."

"Hey, yeah." Menace brightened considerably as he recognized Sam Hyatt's vet truck. The Wesley vet jumped out and Menace started for his truck. "I really gotta get back to the shop, Libby. Call me if you need some help."

"I'll do that," Libby said with a note of irony. Menace didn't slow down as he waved in response.

THE HORSE'S LEG was swollen, just as Kade had said it would be, and he was hurting, so

Libby was glad that Sam had been able to stop by early. The travel costs from Wesley to Otto were going to kill her, though, since Sam's other client had canceled and she'd be paying the entire fee herself. She had a feeling that Sam would waive it, since she'd agreed to go to dinner with him next Saturday night, but she wouldn't let him do that. Libby always kept business and pleasure separate. Life was less complicated that way. It was also less complicated if she kept matters from getting too serious and Sam seemed to understand Libby's emotional boundaries.

"Stan will be back on Monday," Sam said, "but I don't think you'll have any trouble as long as you leave the wound wrapped and keep pouring bute into him." Sam gave the horse a final pat and then let himself out of the pen. "He'll be scarred, though."

"I figured. I just want him healthy."

"He's lucky you found him when you did."

No doubt. Had Cooper spent much longer on his back, he would have died.

"You should have called me," Sam continued as they left the barn and walked the short distance to his dusty utility truck.

"I didn't want to pay an after-hours charge," Libby said with a crooked smile. Sam smiled back and Libby was struck by just how good-looking he was, with his blond hair and blue eyes. Put him in a mackinaw and he'd be the image of a Swedish lumberjack. Shuck him out of that mackinaw—and everything else—and he'd probably be pretty spectacular, too. Libby wasn't yet certain whether she'd ever be doing that.

"We could have worked something out."

"I don't want special treatment," Libby replied, the smile still playing on her lips, possibly because of the mackinaw ruminations.

To her surprise, Sam settled his big hand on her shoulder, his fingers strong and warm. "You might get some anyway."

Her surprise must have shown, because Sam suddenly dropped his hand and busied himself loading his equipment, leaving Libby standing there, feeling… She didn't know how she felt. She liked Sam. And regardless of his good looks, that was where she would leave things for now. The mackinaw would stay on.

"I HEARD YOU'RE getting this place ready to sell." Joe Barton stood with his hands on his hips, surveying the property as Kade threw a saddle onto the chestnut colt's back. It was the second time in a matter of days that Joe had made the forty-mile drive from his ranch to Kade's in order to ride with him.

"There's nothing to keep me here," Kade said. Anything that might have kept him there was far out of reach now.

Joe nodded thoughtfully. "I like the way you handle my colts. I was hoping you'd stay around."

Kade smiled but said nothing. Joe had brought his own horse to ride, another excellent and obviously expensive animal. Kade finished saddling the young horse, then they both mounted and headed off down the county road to the turnoff leading toward the mountains.

Joe was not a natural horseman, but he faked it successfully. The older man watched Kade as he rode, adjusting his body so that his seat was more like Kade's. He didn't ask for advice and Kade never offered any. That was probably why they did so well together.

"We've done some trail work since the last

time we rode," Kade said. "Junior's still learning to carry a load downhill." A young horse had to learn how to sit back on his haunches when being ridden down a steep slope, and sometimes it took a number of tries to teach the lesson.

Joe gave a grunt of acknowledgment, although Kade didn't think he really knew what he was talking about. Well, the first time Joe went over the head of a horse who stumbled because he carried all the weight on his front end, he'd know. Kade's job was to keep that from happening.

"How's your water?" Kade asked. It was a common question in the area, kind of like, "Hot enough for you?"

"Holding out," Joe said. "But I can't sell as much hay this year."

"Feeding it?"

"The BLM won't let me put all my cows on the grazing allotments, so I'm feeding part of the herd year round. They're trying to tell me they're reducing numbers of all animals using the land, but it's a lie."

"How so?"

Joe's jaw tightened. "Because I found out they moved in a herd of mustangs two years ago. They live in the mountains during the summer, but in the winter they come down onto my allotments and eat my grass. When I bought the ranch, I bought the cattle, too. I'd planned on putting the same number out to graze as the previous owner, but this past spring the BLM cut me back by twenty-five percent. Because of the damned mustangs."

"Doesn't seem fair to move a herd in, then cut you back," Kade said, wondering if the herd eating Joe's grass was Blue's herd. It was quite possible. "But you know," he continued, "that's always been mustang country. I'm not sure what happened to the herd that was there before they relocated this one, but there were wild horses in your valley before I was born."

"How do you know?"

Kade smiled. "My grandfather used to ranch in the area. He'd let his horses run with the mustangs when he put them out for the summer. Then he'd gather the whole herd, sort out his horses and let the mustangs go." Most of them, anyway. A few of his grandfather's favorite mounts were mustangs he'd "adopted" on his own. The BLM finally made him stop running his horses with the herd in the 1970s, but he'd told Kade the story many times.

"Yeah? How'd he get his horses back?"

"He built a mustang trap. A classic one, with a long funnel of camouflaged fencing that narrowed down into a hidden corral."

Joe grunted again, and then urged his mount to move faster to keep up with the chestnut. "Prior to buying the Zephyr Valley ranch, I liked wild horses. That was before I was aware of the damage they cause to the range."

Kade debated. Argue with a man who was paying his salary and was convinced he was correct? Or just keep quiet and ride? He chose the middle ground. Diplomacy. "Any animal, in numbers that are too large, can overgraze a range. Usually, in cases like these, the feds cut back on both mustangs and cattle so that there's enough grass. But cattle are easier to regulate."

"The difference between cattle and wild horses is that the government makes a profit from my usage. I'm paying them for the land."

The chestnut suddenly shied, saving Kade from having to reply. He stopped the animal and turned it back. The horse cautiously approached the scary stick lying on the ground, blowing through his nose. Then eventually got close enough to sniff it.

Joe laughed. "I'm always amazed at what will spook a horse."

"Sticks are bad," Kade agreed. Blowing paper was the worst.

The two men headed for home after another twenty minutes, talking about horses as they rode. Joe had always dreamed of breeding horses, and now that he finally had a ranch, he could indulge himself. He was also planning to buy and sell colts, and it sounded as if he was employing the same strategies he'd used to get rich in the stock market. Figure out the bloodlines that should prove most popular in the future. Buy low, sell high. These three colts were his first investments. Kade believed the man had chosen well.

When they got back to the ranch, Joe loaded his horse. Kade went into the trailer and returned with two Cokes.

"Is your house so bad you have to live in your horse trailer?"

Kade said yes with a straight face. And it

was that bad, just not in the sense that Barton meant. Kade figured if the man hung around town at all, he'd eventually hear that Kade and his dad had been estranged, even if he might not learn why.

Not many people knew the truth. Parker Danning had been pretty good at hiding the fact that he hated his only son—in public, anyway. And Kade didn't think anyone knew about that last huge fight, the one where he'd finally fought back for real and proved that he could have taken his father…and then hadn't.

Walking away had been hard, but Kade refused to be his father. He'd moved out that afternoon, into the bunkhouse on Menace's farm, weeks away from his eighteenth birthday. His dad had never come to find him and drag him home as he'd threatened to do in the past when Kade had tried to leave. In fact, his father had never spoken to him again.

"You should probably put a match to it and bring in a double-wide." Joe gestured at the house with the Coke can.

"Tempting." In many ways. "But I can't afford a double-wide." Kade spoke without thinking, then wished he hadn't. His monetary woes were no one else's business.

"If you train enough colts, that could change," Joe said, snapping open the can. "And I will have more that need to be trained, if you're interested."

"I am—for as long as I'm here, anyway."

"I may have to do what I can to see that you stay," Joe said, and Kade had a feeling the guy wasn't being totally facetious.

After the rancher left, Kade fed the four horses, then went into the house to put in a few hours of work. The place felt better now that he'd cleared it out, slapped some paint on the walls. He planned to spend the colt money on flooring, and if a real job didn't materialize shortly he hoped that Barton would send more colts his way. Hell, he could make a fairly reasonable living starting colts, if he didn't mind the uncertainty.

But he did.

He wanted security for once in his life. He'd never had it after his mother had left his abusive dad, effectively abandoning her son when he was twelve. The rodeo life was about as insecure a life as a guy could get, everything hinging on the next big ride. And then, when he finally made it big and thought he had some security, he'd come to find out it was all an illusion because he'd trusted the wrong person. He hadn't been the only one. Dylan Smith had bilked several people out of funds. That didn't make Kade feel one bit less stupid.

THE WESLEY BLM personnel enjoyed four days without Ellen Vargas at the helm, while she represented their office at a state conference. She returned on Friday in a bad mood. Obviously something had not gone as she'd planned.

No one cared to ask, and since there had yet to be a staff meeting summarizing the outcome, a few random theories floated around. But for the most part the crew was simply glad she was leaving them alone. It couldn't last forever, though, and Libby was the one who took the first hit.

"Oh, Libby…"

"Yes, Ellen?" Libby asked politely. She'd been sitting in front of her computer, supposedly working on her report. In actuality she'd been stewing about Kade and her injured horse and what Menace had said about the two of them living in the same community. Again.

"I'd like to see you in my office. Please bring any information you have on the area surrounding the Jessup Creek and Zephyr Valley ranches."

"Zephyr Valley ranch?" Libby had never heard of it before. It certainly wasn't on any of the maps.

"It's the Boggy Flat ranch," Stephen said quietly. Libby turned to stare at him, but he didn't look up—rather like a possum playing dead. Maybe if he didn't move or speak again, Ellen would go away. Fortunately she did, her heels clicking briskly down the hallway.

Stephen straightened up once the coast was clear, removing his glasses and rubbing his eyes. His brown hair was sticking out at weird angles from where he'd been resting his palm on his head as he worked. He'd managed to find another project and he was pouring all of his energy into it in an effort to keep Ellen at bay.

"The Zephyr Valley?" Libby asked. "For real?"

"For real."

Libby shook her head in disgust. What next? The Boggy Flat had been acquired by a wealthy Chicagoan a little more than a year ago, but Libby hadn't known that he'd changed the name of the hundred-year-old ranch.

She opened a file drawer and pulled out the hard copy on the Jessup Valley area before following Ellen into the state's most perfectly appointed office. There was a new flower in the vase. Another orchid.

Ellen waved Libby to a seat. "You're the first person I'm meeting with concerning the conference I just attended. The wild-horse issue was thoroughly discussed and the heads of the other regional offices and I have concluded that we should concentrate our energies on managing the mustang herds grazing on the cattle allotments."

"Manage in what way?" Libby asked. She thought she *was* managing those herds.

"Reducing numbers to a more reasonable level."

"Define reasonable."

"The cattlemen pay for the range, so 'reasonable' would mean the number of horses that can be sustained without affecting the number of cattle that normally graze there."

"What about the deer, elk and antelope?" Libby was fully in support of using the range for cattle, but when the range was in poor condition, everything had to be scaled back.

"Funny you should mention that. According to my research, the mustangs in the Jessup Valley are taking range from native species."

"I'd sure like to see that research."

"I'll see that you get a copy," Ellen said, tidying the stack of papers on her desk as she spoke. "But in the meantime we'll focus on areas that affect the economy."

"And that would be the areas with grazing allotments."

"Exactly. When you finish writing your section of the land-usage report, I want you to address this issue."

"I'll be certain to do that." Libby couldn't keep the sarcasm out of her voice, probably because she wasn't trying very hard to do so.

Ellen set her pen on the desk. "Libby." She folded her hands on the top of her desk and leaned forward. "Let me be blunt, since it's a manner of speaking with which you are quite familiar. Our budget is in trouble. We need the grazing fees, and in addition to that we may have to adjust staff. At the conference we discussed the possibility of sharing personnel over several areas in a cooperative effort. One of the positions discussed was that of wild horse specialist. You have the least seniority."

"I see." Libby refused to let any emotion come into her voice. She had no idea if Ellen was telling her the truth or simply trying to manipulate her, so there was no sense going ballistic over what might well be nothing more than a stretching of the truth.

Ellen adjusted her glasses. "I, of course, fought to keep your position rather than have it absorbed. However, *nothing* is settled yet." She paused. "I will continue to fight for you, as long as I feel you are a benefit to this office." Another pause for effect. *Two, three, four...* "Are we clear on the situation?"

"Very clear." Cooperate with Ellen or walk.

"I want you to look closely at the situation in the Jessup Valley. When you finalize your addition to the usage report, I expect to see suggestions that will take the current economic situation into account."

Libby nodded. She might be hotheaded,

but she wasn't a fool. She'd continue with this game for a while and see how it played out, but damned if she would let this woman force her to include lies in her assessments.

"If that's all?" she asked, holding the folder she'd brought with her in both hands.

"For now," Ellen said. "I look forward to your report."

Libby gave a slight smile and headed for the door.

"Well?" Stephen asked once she returned to their office.

"We have range issues," Libby said shortly.

"Yeah." Stephen leaned back in his chair, propping the sole of his boot on the edge of the desk. "Before Ellen went to the state meeting, she wanted to allow more grazing for the three big ranches in the area. I couldn't recommend increasing time or number of animals on the allotments. Fred agreed with me. She didn't like that much."

"Well," Libby said, thoughtfully twisting a curl around her finger. "She now believes that if she removes the horses from the range, there'll be plenty of food for cattle."

"She's probably right."

"Whose side are you on?"

"Yours. But her thought process makes sense."

"Her thought process is what worries me. And she came back all out of sorts from that meeting, so I'm thinking she got bad news and now she's trying to twist things to get what she wants."

"What *does* she want, Libby?"

"She wants to make friends with some rich ranchers, near as I can tell." Libby shook her head and touched her computer mouse, bringing the screen to life. She had a report to write.

And some thinking to do.

"Do you have plans for the weekend?" Ellen asked later that afternoon as they left the office for the day.

Libby's jaw set at the woman's pretended interest in her staff. The ploy was probably outlined in one of her management books. *Take an interest in your staff. Show them that you care, then carefully insert the knife between the fifth and sixth ribs and twist...*

"Just a long ride in the mountains," Libby said. She dug her keys out of her jacket pocket and started for her truck.

She'd spent as much time contemplating the pros and cons of Menace's advice to suck it up where Kade was concerned as she'd spent debating the mustang situation. She did need to suck it up. It was stupid to think that she could avoid Kade in the tiny community. So why try? Why not just find a middle ground between lovers and enemies? It was the only sane course of action. And it would prove once and for all—to both of them— that there'd never, ever be anything between them again.

And that was why she was going to do more than point out Blue's herd on the map. She would go with Kade to find his horse.

CHAPTER SIX

JOE BARTON WASN'T exactly the man Kade had first thought he was. He'd lived a privileged life and had only a passing familiarity with the word *no,* but he also worked hard. He didn't leave everything for his underlings to take care of. Kade had a feeling that had their positions been reversed, Barton would not have been fleeced out of his fortune by a no-good accountant; he would have been well aware of everything that was happening with his money. Kade had been trusting and oblivious, learning the hard way that people who said they were your friends still had to be watched.

Kade was not only learning to like Joe, he was thankful he had the three colts to train, because the job offers weren't exactly pouring in. He really hadn't expected to get hired on at the Lone Eagle Mine, but he'd thought he might have had a shot at a couple of the jobs advertised in Wesley—driving a propane delivery truck or doing day labor at the aggregate plant. He hadn't even been asked for an interview. Apparently bronc busting—even world-class bronc busting— wasn't enough of a skill to make the short list for those kinds of positions.

Sheri hadn't called, either, since that one excited phone exchange a couple of weeks ago, so obviously the Rough Out endorsement deal was down the tubes. Kade felt no surprise. He hadn't been easy to deal with when he'd been drunk, and he'd been stupid and arrogant enough to think that he could do as he pleased and a major advertiser would still want him to work for them. After all, sales of Rough Out jeans had jumped when he'd been used in their print ads. Difficult was difficult, however, and he'd pulled one too many no-shows on them, due to rotten hangovers.

Stupid, stupid, stupid.

But drunks weren't known for making well-thought-out, informed decisions. He'd instinctively stayed away from Maddie during those months, not wanting his kid to see him in that state, and telling himself he'd get sober and make it up to her tomorrow.

Jillian had made no waves about him not seeing Maddie. She'd liked that Kade no longer upset their daughter's controlled existence. But then he'd had a rude awakening when the IRS contacted him, wanting a whole lot of money because his accountant, the one Jillian had warned him about, hadn't bothered to pay his taxes. Instead, Dylan Smith had pocketed the money and taken off for Brazil or some such country while Kade was left holding the bag. The big, empty bag. It had taken almost everything he had left to settle that debt, but at least it had sobered him up once and for all.

And then, when he realized he'd missed months of his kid's life, and had no way to support her, he'd set about becoming the kind of person, the kind of dad, he wanted to be.

"Would you be interested in taking on some more colts?" Barton asked him out of the blue as they rode through the sage toward a trail leading to the mountains.

"Yes," Kade responded. No sense playing coy.

"There's just one thing."

Kade glanced over at Barton, whose tone had changed. "What's that?"

"I'll want you under contract. I don't want

to invest in colts and then not have a trainer whose name will help sell them."

"So I'd be guaranteed employment." That would be nice. He nudged the colt to keep him from pausing to eat the tall crested wheat growing between the sage bushes.

"And I'd be guaranteed that you won't sell your ranch and quit the country."

"How long a contract?" Because he fully intended to sell the ranch and quit the country as soon as he could.

"I want sixty days put on the colts I sell, with an option to re-up for a longer period if we're both happy with the deal."

"That sounds reasonable." It would take longer than sixty days to settle all the issues involved in selling the ranch once he found a buyer. And, if he was able to move to Elko after the sale, he could continue to work for Joe, since the town wasn't far away by Nevada standards. Yes. A renewable contract was sounding better and better.

"You aren't drinking anymore, are you." It was a statement, not a question, and Kade wasn't surprised that Barton had investigated his background.

"No."

"And you wouldn't have a problem coming over to the ranch and meeting some people, maybe show off what you've done with the colts you're breaking in now?"

"Nope."

"I'll have my lawyer draw up a contract."

Kade and Joe talked bloodlines for the rest of the ride, taciturn Joe growing more enthusiastic as he picked Kade's brain. Kade felt remarkably optimistic himself when Joe finally drove his shiny truck and horse trailer down the driveway—until he went into his own trailer and listened to the voice message from his ex-wife asking him to call.

Sensing the worst, he punched in her number. The news wasn't terrible, but it wasn't that great, either. Jillian had planned a family trip for the next weekend, *his* weekend, and Maddie wanted to go.

What could he say?

He had several things he *wanted* to say, but Jillian jumped in first.

"Mike and I will bring Maddie down next weekend to make up for it. No travel."

"Are you sure you're not going to plan another big event that Maddie can't possibly miss the next weekend?"

"If you want her to come this weekend, she will. It's up to you."

Kade took a few paces across the trailer, attempting to keep his temper in check. "You've got to stop doing this, Jill."

"I'm not doing anything except trying to keep Maddie's life stable."

"I'm aware," Kade said. "Gotta go." He hung up the phone before he could say anything Jillian could use against him and then slammed his palm against the storage cabinet beside the stove.

He needed to sell the ranch and get back up to Elko. He hoped Jason's wife would call him soon.

KADE'S PHONE KEPT kicking into voice mail, so Libby pulled into his driveway on her way home.

No time like the present to start practicing the new role she'd assigned herself—that of a civil acquaintance. Another name for it would be ex-lover-who-hates-living-in-the-same-community-but-is-determined-to-save-face.

The door to the house hung wide open.

Libby sat in her truck for a moment before

getting out, wondering if Kade's daughter would be there again. But at three o'clock on a Friday afternoon the girl should just be getting out of school in Elko. Or so Libby hoped.

She crossed the weedy gravel to the house, the sound of hammering growing louder as she approached.

"Hello?" she called as she entered the nearly empty kitchen, remembering the many times she'd done so in the past—usually when Kade's dad was away from the place.

The hammering stopped abruptly and Kade appeared at the end of the hall, wearing a sweaty T-shirt that clung to his chest, out-lining his muscles. Libby swallowed and reminded herself of her role. Civil acquaintance.

She cleared her throat. "Uh, hi," she said, now aware that "civil acquaintance" was going to be a lot more difficult than "angry ex." Anger felt safe because it kept the emotions high and protected her from having to acknowledge that she still found Kade ridiculously attractive, that she could close her eyes and remember how it felt to smooth her hands over his muscles, feel his lips on her skin.

"Hi," he echoed. For a moment they stared at one another, his questioning hazel eyes meeting her cautious blue ones.

Libby squared her shoulders then, as if preparing for a fight. "I came to tell you that I changed my mind. I will go with you to find Blue."

His expression didn't change. "Why?"

Libby blinked at him. "The polite thing to say is 'thank you.' I'm off tomorrow. Does that work for you?"

"Works fine."

"If I'm intruding on some plans…"

"No."

"Are you alone this weekend?"

"Alone?"

"Will your daughter be coming with us?" she asked with more of an edge to her voice than she'd intended.

"I won't get to see her again for a week or so."

"Oh." She tried not to sound relieved, but she was. Riding with Kade, like old times, would be hard enough without having a walking, talking reminder of his infidelity along.

"Whose trailer shall we take?"

"We can take the old stock trailer."

"Good. The road's bad and I don't want to beat up mine."

Kade smiled slightly. "We could borrow Menace's father's trailer and get it back before he realizes it's gone."

"Maybe next time." Libby smiled back, then remembered herself. Acquaintance, not coconspirator. "What time do you want me here?"

"I could swing by and pick you up at your place."

"My trailer's already hitched. It's no problem driving over." And she wanted to stay in control of her comings and goings.

"Why don't we leave here at about 4:00 a.m.?"

Libby's lower jaw shifted sideways. "You're pushing things. You know that."

There was still a hint of humor in his eyes as he said, "Yeah, Lib. I do."

"I'll be here at five. I have a date tomorrow night, so I want to get back early."

After a slight pause he said, "Fine."

"All right." Libby felt oddly self-conscious, which made her tone brusque as she added, "See you tomorrow."

"See you tomorrow. Hey, Lib," he called, since she was already halfway out the door. She turned back, one had on the door frame. "How's your horse?"

"Better. The swelling's going down and there's no infection."

He smiled that smile she'd loved so much once upon a time. "I'm glad to hear that. See you tomorrow."

BOTH THE HOUSE and the horse trailer were dark when Libby pulled into Kade's driveway. She parked the truck and waited, but there was no sign of life. She no longer needed to be home early, since Sam had called the night before to postpone their date—he had to cover for another vet in Elko—but Libby saw no reason to tell Kade that. She wanted to hold on to that excuse for getting back.

So where was Kade? Libby got out of the truck, zipping her sweatshirt against the crisp morning air. He lived in the trailer, so she'd start there. Was he still in bed? If he was, she hoped he no longer slept in the nude.

Libby shoved the image out of her mind as she approached the side door. Kade's trailer was top-of-the-line, with fancy living quarters in the front and room for three horses in the rear. It was shiny and well kept up, except for the area on the side where there had once been writing. The words had been painted over, but Libby could make out the outlines of the raised letters. *Kade Danning, World Champion Saddle Bronc Rider.*

Libby hadn't been around for his glory days. He'd become a world champion PB— Post Breakup, or Post Betrayal. Either one worked for her. The media had loved him, though, so she still got a healthy dose of Kade, like it or not. Not long after the second world title, the one he'd won after coming back from a serious injury, Libby had been bombarded by his image on billboards and in magazines, selling Dusty Saddle microbrew and Rough Out jeans. Women loved him and men admired him. Libby had hated his guts by then, because he had lied to her in the worst possible way. It had taken her a long time to get to the point where seeing his image didn't send a sharp stab of pain through her or piss her off. And now she was about to spend the day with him voluntarily.

She was growing. It wasn't easy, but she was making progress.

Kade came around the barn then, leading a beautiful chestnut colt with a lot of chrome—four high white socks and a wide blaze down his face.

Libby let out a low whistle.

"He's not mine," Kade said before loading the horse into the beat-up stock trailer.

"Whose horse is he?"

"Joe Barton's."

"The guy who owns the Boggy Flat ranch?" Libby asked.

"Zephyr Valley."

Libby was glad to hear the note of sarcasm in Kade's voice.

"Tell me about him," Libby said before disappearing into her own trailer and unloading her horse, a sturdy gray mare named Mouse. "Barton, I mean. All I know is he's some rich guy from Chicago."

"I don't know much more than that about him. I'm putting miles on some colts for him."

"No big political connections or anything?"

"I have no idea. Why?"

"Just wondering." It had occurred to her that Ellen's drive to rid the range of mustangs might be a maneuver to gain political favor; she could be doing a favor for someone influential in order to advance her career. Not too ethical, but if she was slick enough about it, it would be hard to prove.

Kade studied her, a slight frown creasing his forehead. No, she would not share her concerns with Kade. Once upon a time, yes, but not now.

Kade took Mouse's lead rope and loaded her into his stock trailer next to the colt. The colt tried to get friendly and the mare flattened her ears.

"She's as cranky as you are," Kade said.

"You want company on this trip?"

Kade stepped out of the trailer and shut the door. "You know I do." His voice was low and intimate. Libby's belly tightened at the sound. At the memory of that voice in her ear, telling her what he wanted to do before he went ahead and did it.

She walked up to the truck and climbed inside. It smelled of Kade. She felt like leaning her hot forehead against the cool glass of the window.

Civil acquaintance. Civil acquaintance.

ONCE THEY'D REACHED the trailhead and
unloaded the already saddled horses, Kade
mounted easily, displaying none of the stiff-
ness that bronc riders tended to show as they
aged.

"Ready?" He was already looking up the
trail, his strong profile sharply contrasted
against the pale apricot sky.

"Yeah."

Technically, she should have been leading
the way since she was the guide, but Libby
didn't mind being behind him. It gave her a
barrier as she recalled all the times they'd
ridden in the mountains as teens—escaping
together. She remembered the good times
and felt cheated that things had turned out as
they had.

*You're here to find a horse, not to whine
about the past.*

Libby straightened in the saddle, focused
on the mission. She'd seen Blue three times
since she and Kade had released him, all in
an official capacity. The first time Libby
had checked on Blue's herd, almost ten
years after his release, she hadn't expected
to find the stud still alive, figuring that a
domestic horse probably would have

perished due to the harsh conditions in which mustangs lived. But no. He'd not only survived, he'd thrived. His herd was about half roan, blues, reds and even a few lilacs. And thankfully they were remote, rarely monitored or gathered.

It wasn't until the valley had burned two years ago that she'd dealt with the herd again. There'd been no adoptions, since the herd was small and healthy. Because of Glen and his dislike of bureaucracy, they'd simply moved the herd to another valley. No red tape, no protocol. For all Libby knew, Glen hadn't even had the authority to make such a move. She'd never asked because she preferred not knowing. The important thing was that the herd was located in a place where they could find adequate range.

Libby followed Kade for more than an hour before urging Mouse ahead to catch up with him.

"They could be in any one of these drainages," she said. "We released them lower in the valley and they migrated up these drainages for the feed. They go lower in the winter, of course." Too low, since the herd had intruded on grazing allotments and now a rich man wasn't happy about that.

Too bad for the rich man.

THEY CRESTED A LOW, sage-covered ridge and rode into yet another drainage when Kade pulled his horse to a stop. Below them they saw a herd, maybe forty-strong. And more than half of them were roans. Blue had done his job. Kade pulled a small pair of binoculars out of his shirt pocket and trained them on the herd, which, having caught sight of them, started to move. The lead mare had a nice new bay baby by her side, and there, traveling beside the strung-out mares, was a stocky red roan, the spitting image of Blue, except for the color.

But no Blue.

Kade frowned as he scanned the horses. Several blue roans, but none large and sturdy enough to be his horse. He gave a start when Libby touched his sleeve.

He followed the direction she was pointing, then lifted the binoculars.

"Oh, damn," he murmured. There was Blue, a good two or three hundred yards behind the herd, alone. Limping slightly. And skinny. Very skinny.

"I think his son might be taking the herd away from him," Libby said.

"Yeah." Kade could think of nothing better to say. He'd been prepared for the possibility that he wouldn't find Blue with the herd. Accidents happened in the wild. But he hadn't been prepared to see his horse struggling behind the herd, trying to keep up with the band he had once led.

And then, as if on cue, the younger stud charged back, threatening Blue, who stopped, tried to turn on his haunches and went down due to his bad back leg. The red roan stopped, having made his point, and returned to the flank of the herd. The mares continued on down the canyon as if nothing had happened, the lead mare disappearing around a corner and into the aspens that grew along the creek as Blue hefted himself to his feet again.

Blue followed determinedly along behind them. When he disappeared from sight, Kade lowered the glasses.

"I'm sorry," Libby said quietly. No other words followed.

Kade swallowed and then gave his head one sad shake before turning his horse around on the trail. When his knee came even with Libby's, he met her eyes. Yeah, she felt for him.

"He probably had a better life out here than he'd have had with my old man," Kade said. And it was true. The old man never would have sold Blue, since the stud had impeccable breeding and he could have gotten some healthy stud fees out him, totally ignoring the fact that the stud had been a gift to Kade from his grandfather just before he'd passed away.

"No doubt," she said impassively.

It would have been better to make this discovery alone, but if someone had to be with him, he was glad it was Libby. "Let's go," he said.

They made their way back down the trail, and now that the horses sensed they were heading for the trailer, they picked up their pace.

It's the way it has to be. It's the way life ends for a stallion in the wild. Pushed away from his herd by a younger horse. Blue had undoubtedly done the same to the herd's previous stallion.

But logic and common sense didn't ease the picture of Blue going down and then limping after the herd. Kade doubted anything would.

LIBBY RECOGNIZED THE effort Kade was putting into keeping his face expressionless. Matter-of-fact. But the sixteen-year-old kid in him, the one who'd loved this horse so much that he'd set him free, had to be dying inside right now.

The ride back took forever, despite the horses' faster gaits, and Libby was relieved to see the truck and trailer sitting on the road below when they came over the final ridge.

Almost over. Duty almost done. And then she could go back to her place and get on with her life. She had problems of her own to sort out. Kade wasn't one of them. And except in a professional capacity, neither was Blue. She couldn't do a thing for either of them.

It was a long drive home. They were both tired and Kade remained quiet. Preoccupied. Neither of them spoke until he pulled into the driveway.

Kade turned off the ignition and then once again Libby said, "Sorry about Blue."

"I knew what I was getting into when I decided to find him."

He might have known, but he hadn't been prepared.

Neither of them made a move to get out of the truck. Kade leaned his elbow against the door, propping his head on his hand as he stared at the sorry old house.

"What now, Kade?" Libby asked softly. She'd thought he'd talk about Blue, but he didn't.

"I'm selling as soon as I get it into some kind of selling shape."

Good. She was almost ashamed of the thought. Almost. But it *would* make her life so much easier if he just left. "Why not sell it as is? There's a market."

"I have to get as much out of it as I can." He continued to stare at the house, his expression troubled, as if he expected his dad to come bursting out of it at any moment.

Libby opened the truck door, but she didn't climb out. "Because of the IRS?" She'd heard the rumor that he was stone broke because of back taxes. And even though it was none of her business she couldn't help but wonder what he'd done with all his money, why he hadn't had enough to pay his taxes. Had he gambled his money away? Drunk it away? Did his ex-wife have most of it?

She wasn't going to ask.

"I settled that debt, but I had to sell almost everything I owned. Now I need enough money to tide me over while I get some job training. Apparently there's not a lot of call for washed-up rodeo cowboys in today's job market."

Divorced, broke and unskilled. Quite a résumé.

"Has anything gone right for you?" Libby asked without thinking.

"Yeah." He glanced up at her then, his expression surprisingly intense. She'd seen that look before, couldn't believe she was seeing it now, and tried to convince herself she wasn't by playing it cool.

"What's that?"

"You're not married."

It took Libby a moment to assure herself she'd heard correctly. She pulled in a deep breath. "There will never be anything between us, Kade. I mean it."

"I know you do."

"Then you'd better damned well believe me."

"Oh, trust me, Lib. I do."

She didn't believe *him*. Not when he was wearing his determined face, the one he'd worn whenever he was facing a particularly challenging bronc.

She gave him a long hard stare before saying what was in her heart. "I might feel for you, Kade, but the very *last* thing I will ever do in this life is trust you."

CHAPTER SEVEN

YOU'RE NOT MARRIED. Kade had no idea why he'd said that, but it was true. He was glad Libby wasn't married. That didn't mean he thought he had a chance with her—it had been a flat-ass stupid thing to say and now she had her back up again, just when it had looked as if they might be on the healing road.

But deep down, maybe he *wanted* her to have her back up. Maybe he preferred that to indifference.

No maybe about it. He did prefer it to indifference.

Well, Libby had been anything but indifferent when she left today. She'd been steamed and had left no illusions to the contrary. It had taken her almost three minutes to unload her horse from his trailer, load the mare into her own and drive away.

And as he thought about it, Kade realized he wasn't all that unhappy about saying what he'd said. Sometimes a guy had to speak from the heart.

YOU'RE NOT MARRIED.

One whole day had passed and Libby was still pissed off that Kade had said such a thing. She frowned down at the industrial-gray floor tiles in the break room.

"Ahem." Stephen got up from the long table where he'd been eating his lunch and tossed his wadded-up paper bag in the trash. "What's going on?"

"What do you mean?"

"You seem, oh, I don't know, preoccupied?"

Libby frowned. "Why do you say that?"

"You've been standing there stirring your coffee for about five minutes, staring at the floor."

"So?"

He pointed at her cup. "You didn't put anything in your coffee to stir."

Libby looked down. Sure enough. No creamer. "Old habits," she said, gamely sipping the coffee black and somehow managing not to make a face. She hated coffee without cream.

"You gave up creamer?" Stephen asked dubiously.

"Too much palm oil."

"Right." Stephen boosted himself onto the counter, the backs of his boots clunking on the cabinet doors.

Libby gave him a narrow-eyed appraisal. "I'll bet there's something in the rule book about that. I just can't believe having your butt on the counter is correct protocol."

"Yeah? Well, Queenie can—"

A door opened and closed out in the hall and Stephen's mouth snapped shut. Libby smirked at him as hc got off the counter.

"On second thought, it's not worth crossing her."

"I hear you," Libby said, although she believed that crossing Ellen was inevitable. "I've got a few more items to finish up on my report."

When Libby started down the hall, Ellen was coming back down the hall from the copy room.

"Did you enjoy your weekend, Libby?"

"It was great," Libby said before walking

into her office and shutting the door, something she'd rarely done when Glen had been her boss.

She brought up her word-processing screen, put her hands on the keyboard and stared at the computer, her concentration shot because of Ellen's inquiry.

Oh, yeah. Her weekend had been great— right up until they'd found Blue injured and limping behind his herd. And then Kade had had to top things off by making that comment. She'd give him this—he had balls. To say something like that after what he'd done… She'd never questioned his integrity when they'd been together, and it had ripped her world apart when she found he'd slept with another woman.

And truthfully, she'd been devastated almost as much by her own naiveté and blindness as by his screwing around. She'd felt foolish. So the bottom line was that she couldn't trust him, and she couldn't trust her own judgment. What kind of a basis was that for anything?

"ARE THERE ANY KIDS around where you live?" Maddie asked when Kade called to make plans for her next visit, which was coming up soon.

Kade hadn't thought about that. Of course Maddie would want to play with other kids. Jason and Kira had a year-old baby boy, Matt, but that wasn't what Maddie had in mind.

"I'm sure there're some kids here."

"With horses?"

"I'll, uh, have to ask around."

So he did. He didn't find any kids with horses, but he learned there was a weekend craft class at the public library and a family swim at the community pool. Both good places to meet other kids. He signed Maddie up for the next class, which was lanyard braiding, paying the small fee. He didn't know who had kids and who didn't, so he also called the woman who'd run the 4-H program back when he'd been in it and found out she was still in charge. Maddie couldn't join a club, but she could attend the local horse group as a guest.

Three for three. Kade went home feeling like a real dad. And he actually had the house to the point where they could stay in it if she wanted to, although he had a feeling she'd want to stay in the trailer. If she ever wanted to become a rodeo rider, she was more than prepared for the lifestyle—news that wouldn't exactly thrill her mother.

The phone rang that afternoon and Kade assumed he'd be passing good news along to Maddie, but instead, he received an invitation to an afternoon soiree Joe Barton was holding, along with a request to bring Joe's three colts with him—if he wouldn't mind. Kade didn't mind. Some time away from the house would be welcome.

"I'd like to have you meet some people and firm up a few things."

"Sure," Kade said. "Uh…how dressy is this event?"

"Wear your regular clothes. Jeans. Boots. Hat. It's very casual. I might have you put that Appaloosa through his paces. I have a potential buyer."

"No problem. See you tomorrow."

THE BOGGY FLAT RANCH had a new sign arching over the entryway, announcing it as the Zephyr Valley ranch. Intricate silhouettes of cattle and cowboys on horseback adorned the top of the iron arch. It gave an excellent first impression and Kade had a feeling that first impressions were important to Joe Barton.

As Kade drove to the formerly run-down main ranch, he could see that more changes were in progress. A pivot was irrigating land that had lain fallow for a long, long time, and a nice herd of Angus grazed in the upper pasture. He knew from their last ride together that Barton was champing at the bit, wanting to get more cattle out on the allotments. He was ticked off that some of the other ranches had been allowed more animals than he'd been allowed, and when Kade had explained that it had more to do with the condition of the range than anything else, Barton had made a disparaging remark.

Kade honestly couldn't decide how he felt about the guy. In some respects, he really liked him, enjoyed riding with him and talking to him about life. Every now and again it made him think about how he and his father should have been.

But then the hard-nosed businessman would appear, stubborn about wanting his way regardless, and Kade would keep his mouth shut rather than argue. He was, after all, an employee, and even today, while visiting the ranch, it was more a command performance than friendship. Joe wanted to show off his new colt trainer. And Kade, wanting food on the table and a new floor in the house, went, telling himself it was just business, letting himself be shown off like a prize stallion.

When he drove up, there were people standing on the lawn, holding drinks and talking. Joe came to greet him and signaled to one of his cowboys to unload the colts. The man immediately hopped to.

"Kade, good to see you." He glanced down at Kade's belt to see if he'd worn one of his big buckles. Kade hadn't. It was one thing to wear them for a photo shoot, another to wear them to impress people. The buckles were damned huge and uncomfortable. Instead, he'd worn one of his favorites from a small rodeo he'd competed in before going pro.

Joe accompanied Kade onto the lawn, where he met a legislator, a doctor, two lawyers, a couple of businessmen and several other people who didn't announce their occupations or social standing. All were dressed in trendy western clothing, the kind most real ranchers and cowboys couldn't afford. Joe made certain everyone knew that Kade, the only person there wearing a plain white shirt and jeans, including Joe's cowboys, was a world champ.

"Kade starts my colts," he announced. "After lunch he'll show us the three he's been working with." The people nodded politely and Kade hoped that Joe didn't expect him to put on too much of a show.

The conversation turned to ranch animals, and Kade continued to sip his drink and blend into the scenery. Joe was probably disappointed that he wasn't taking a more active role in the conversation, but he was *there,* and Joe would have to make do with that.

"You don't have as many cows as I thought you'd have," one of the businessmen noted.

"I'll be getting more," Joe said, "just as soon as I get the range I need." Joe nodded at the woman he'd introduced as a lawyer— Jodie something—as if he expected her to do something about it.

"Federal ground is multiple use," she said coolly, giving Kade a speculative look over the top of her drink. The woman had money written all over her, from the top of her classy blond head to the bottom of her fancy, handmade, red-leather cowboy boots.

"And I'm all for that," Joe said. "Hunting, recreation vehicles, whatever. I just don't understand why those damned horses get to graze my allotments all year long, and I pay the price. Why not limit their usage?"

Several people nodded sagely, but not the lawyer. "Wild horses were here before your cows," she pointed out with a small smile before once again coolly sipping her drink, waiting for a response.

"They're not wild. They're feral," the doctor responded.

"They're 'national treasures,'" Joe added sarcastically. His foreman, a genuine wannabe cowboy if Kade had ever seen one, smirked at the comment. Kade drank his overly sugared iced tea and listened to the conversation, thinking how Libby would have livened it up. She would have set them straight on feral versus wild, and just which animals had what rights and why.

And she probably would have mentioned something about people moving in from out of state and then expecting the rules to be changed for them because they were so darned important. He imagined she'd also be wearing those snug jeans she'd had on at the bar and a shirt that showed her curves. While he was imagining, he figured he might as well aim high.

Kade leaned against a newel post and watched the interplay between the guests, wondering how long he'd be able to keep his mouth shut.

For a while, probably. For Maddie. For his fiscal well-being.

"You were a rodeo rider," the lawyer said as she moved to stand beside him. He caught the scent of a light floral perfume. The same scent Sheri wore.

"I was," Kade agreed.

"What do rodeo riders do after they retire?"

"Ache a lot."

She smiled, showing beautiful white teeth. There wasn't anything about her that wasn't polished and perfect.

"How do you know Joe?" Kade asked.

"He's my father."

Kade was surprised. Apparently the daughter had no qualms about publicly contradicting her father. Like father, like daughter. "So you know him well." Kade swirled the ice in his glass.

She smiled again. "He's happy with what you're doing with the colts."

"Glad to hear it."

"If you go into business with him, I think *you'll* be quite happy." She raised her eyebrows significantly. "I think I might be happy, too."

He glanced down at her hand. Even though her name was not Barton, she wore no ring.

"Divorced," she said, following his gaze.

Kade refrained from telling her he was single. All his instincts were advising him to tread lightly.

"How about you?" she asked.

"Involved," he lied, making it easier on both of them.

"That's not good news."

He shrugged.

Lunch was served shortly thereafter and then Kade put the colts through their paces, wishing Joe had planned the dog-and-pony show before lunch so he could have gotten out of there sooner. It hadn't taken long for Kade to figure out that the other guests, perhaps with the exception of Joe's daughter, considered him to be a subspecies—interesting, perhaps, but not one of them. And they weren't stingy with the condescending attitudes. Nope. There were plenty of those to go around. But in the end, Kade decided the afternoon had been worthwhile, since two of the men there were interested in buying Barton's high-priced colts, which made his future employment that much more secure.

"Thanks for coming," Joe said as he walked with Kade to his truck and trailer, which looked decidedly shabby next to the assortment of fancy pickups and SUVs parked along the fence. The colts were already loaded and ready to go back.

"Thanks for showing me off," Kade replied.

"Hey," Joe said, unfazed, "that's part of being in this business. I thought you were used to being in the public eye."

"I got tired of it," Kade said.

"Then why is that agent of yours pursuing endorsements?"

How do you know that?

But Kade knew how. And why. Guys like Barton didn't become money guys because they were generous and trusting.

"What else have you dug up?"

"You drank your way out of your endorsements, you've been sober for more than a year and your chances at getting another endorsement deal are just about nil. You've been out of the limelight for too long."

"Then I'm not much of an asset to you."

"You're wrong. The people I plan to sell to want horse expertise and pizzazz. You can provide both."

"But will I?"

"Yes. I think you will." He spoke confidently, but not patronizingly. It was more a simple, matter-of-fact statement. "It'll be a mutually beneficial partnership, Kade."

Kade nodded. It would be beneficial, but he had his limits. "I don't want to do any more things like today. Talk me up all you want and I'll show off the colts, but I won't do more of this meet-and-greet stuff."

Joe looked as if he wanted to argue, but he must have sensed that Kade could only be pushed so far.

"Agreed."

LIBBY WAS WORRIED about her mustangs. She had the definite feeling that political clout would end up being far more powerful than her recommendation, which was to leave the herd at its current size, gathering only when the numbers increased by thirty percent, and that the number of cattle on the allotment should remain the same. She was not changing that recommendation. It was based on two years of data and dead on, whether it was what Ellen wanted to hear or not.

Her injured horse, Cooper, was becoming antsy from being confined in his pen, and he let his impatience be known by getting pushy with Libby when she tried to doctor him.

"Knock it off," Libby growled when he knocked her sideways for the third time as she worked to tape the bandage into place.

"Need help?"

Libby jumped at the sound of Kade's voice, then brushed the curls back off her forehead. "I didn't hear you drive in."

"The dogs met me." And the traitors were indeed glued to his sides right now, their eyes trained on Libby.

"I was concentrating on the horse. He wants out of here."

She continued to work, cursing when the

horse bumped her again and the tape doubled back on itself.

"He's moving better," Kade agreed.

"Yes. We're both looking forward to him getting back out on the pasture," she said as she fought to unstick the layers of tape, then gave up and started with a new piece. She peeled it off successfully and set to work.

Kade watched without saying a word, making her a zillion times more aware of him than she should have been.

"So," Libby finally said, shoving her hair back from her forehead again as she straightened and wishing she'd pulled it back with a rubber band, "what brings you here?"

"I have questions. Professional ones."

Her taut muscles relaxed slightly. "Shoot."

"I've been talking to Joe Barton. He seems to think the BLM will be gathering mustangs near his allotments."

"I don't *think* so," Libby said in an insulted tone. "If they are, it's news to me." *Damn it. What was Ellen up to now?*

"Okay, then, hypothetically, if you ever did gather Blue's herd, what are the chances of him being put up for adoption?"

And then she understood. He wanted Blue.

She wished she had a more positive answer than the one she was about to give him. "An older stallion? Not good." She let herself out of the pen, even though she was tempted to keep some metal between the two of them.

"Even though he's infirm?"

"Even less likely." Libby slipped the ring of tape over her wrist like a bracelet, then closed up the vet kit and stowed it against the wall. She started out of the barn and Kade followed, closing the door behind him. Libby purposely kept walking toward Kade's truck. He might be there to get answers, but there was no reason he couldn't be on his way once he got them.

"Let's say there's someone who'll give him a home, like, say, me."

Libby let out a sigh. "If I make specific recommendations as to mustang adoption, even if they make sense, the powers that be won't listen to them. There was a scandal a few years back, with federal employees earmarking the best horses for friends and relatives to adopt. Anything that even hints at that is frowned upon. And let me tell you, my new boss hates me, so anything I suggest that's out of the ordinary is sure to be shot down."

"Your outfit doesn't make things easy, does it?"

"Protocol," Libby muttered. "New sheriff in town and she ain't friendly."

"I see." Kade shoved his thumbs in his front pockets. "I want Blue back. He won't make it through next winter, the shape he's in." Kade was wearing that stubborn expression again.

Libby gave him a hard look. "You aren't thinking of doing something dumb, are you?"

"Like?"

"Robbing a government herd."

He cocked his head. "It's not robbing if you own the animal."

"It is if you can't prove he's yours."

"Worried about me?" he asked softly, his gaze sliding to her lips.

"Yeah," she said sardonically. "Because if they locked you up, I might never see you again."

"Libby…" he said in that same low voice, not at all deterred by her sarcasm. Her name came out like a caress.

"Damn it, Kade. Stop it."

He pulled his gaze back to her eyes. "I'm sorry I hurt you."

And she was sorry that he was giving her that look, the one that used to make her insides go liquid. "That's great, Kade. But it doesn't make it all better."

"If I go and get Blue, will you turn me in?"

The quick change of topic threw her off balance. "Maybe."

He took a step closer. "No, you won't."

Libby raised her chin. "How do you know?"

He took her face in his warm, work-roughened hands and, heaven help her, Libby did not take that important step back. The one she had to take if she wanted to keep their relationship the way it was. He lowered his mouth to hers, kissed her. Slowly. Deeply.

It felt so familiar, so welcome, so hot, that it was a few seconds before Libby shoved against his chest, knocking him back against his truck. She spun around and stalked to the house without a word, wiping the back of her hand across her mouth as she went. Erasing the sensation.

The rest of the evening was shot and Libby eventually gave up and went to bed early. To her lonely bed. She was tired of being alone. And Kade was not the answer.

LIBBY MET SAM after work on Friday night for their dinner date. Since he'd just come off an emergency call, his blond hair was rumpled and he wore jeans and a plaid shirt. She wore her field khakis and a black T-shirt. They made a striking couple when they walked into the Supper Club, Wesley's finest dining facility, because they were the most underdressed couple there.

Over drinks, Sam told her vet stories, which Libby always found entertaining since she understood animals almost as well as, and in some ways better than, he did. The restaurant started to fill up after their main course arrived, and Libby was glad they'd opted to go out early.

"You never told me you were friends with Kade Danning," Sam said.

Libby stared at him over what had been a fairly decent steak—until then.

"I guess I didn't see any reason to." Sam, who was normally quite intelligent, didn't take the hint.

"I used to love to watch him ride."

"He was good," Libby said, picking up her glass of water, sipping.

"I thought it was a shame, what happened to him."

"You mean when that horse almost did him in?"

"No. The IRS. Losing everything."

"Hey, you don't pay your taxes, they come looking for you," Libby said coldly. She did not want to talk about Kade. Not after Saturday.

"I heard he got screwed by his financial guy."

How was it that Sam knew more about Kade than she did?

"He drank his way into a lot of trouble, too," Libby said harshly. "I read it in *People* magazine."

"All the same…"

Libby wadded up her napkin and dropped it on the table before placing a palm on either side of her plate and leaning forward. "Look, Kade and I didn't stay in touch over the years, so I don't know that much about him anymore, but if you want his number I'm sure I can get it for you."

"No, I don't…." Sam put his hand on Libby's arm, and after staring at it for a moment, she leaned back in her seat, her shoulders slumping as she glanced away. She was embarrassed at her response to what were really just innocent questions and comments. "I didn't mean to upset you."

"And I didn't mean to overreact." Libby shook her curls back over her shoulders as she met Sam's gaze. "We were more than friends. It ended badly."

"Oh." The word was delivered self-consciously. "I didn't know. Sorry." He cast her a sideways glance. "Want to call it a night?"

Yes.

"No, I don't want to go yet." Be alone. Brood. She'd done enough of that lately, about both Kade and her upcoming presentation to Ellen.

"Good." He reached across the table and touched her fingers lightly.

Libby forced a smile, then picked up her napkin and flattened it out. She could see Sam had more questions, but fortunately he refrained from asking them. The rest of the evening went well, and Sam walked Libby to her truck.

"I had a nice time," Libby said. And she had.

"I kind of thought…"

Libby shook her head. "No worries."

Then, on impulse, she took his face in her hands and kissed him. It was…pleasant. Just as she'd feared.

Why wouldn't her damned toes curl when she really needed them to?

CHAPTER EIGHT

LIBBY KNEW SHE'D BE making another trip to Ellen's office as soon as her boss read her portion of the land-usage report. Libby had not only made a recommendation to leave the mustang herd size unchanged, but she backed her claim with evidence of historical range usage.

Approximately fifteen years earlier, during a jump in beef prices, the Boggy Flat ranch had started grazing almost double the amount of cattle they once had, and that was about the time the mustang herd had disappeared from the Jessup Valley allotment area. Libby had no information about why the herd had disappeared, whether it was the result of too much competition for grass or perhaps an infectious disease. There were many possibilities, and since she had no way of knowing the truth she wasn't about to point fingers.

The Jessup Valley range had been stable and viable back when Glen had authorized the relocation of the mustang herd to that area. There had been plenty of grass for both the Boggy Flat cattle and the horses.

The following two winters had been dry, however, and allotment grazing times had been cut across the northern part of the state. But looking at the overall numbers, there were no more horses than before; in fact, there were fewer, due to the contraception program. Therefore a gather was not a reasonable option. Nor was relocation.

The current mustang herd was only half the size of the previous one, and Joe Barton was still allowed to graze twenty-five percent more cattle than had been grazed fifteen years ago. All in all, Libby thought it was fair usage for all factions involved, considering the condition of the land.

Ellen would not be happy. Libby was creating a professional nightmare for herself, but she had no other option except to roll over and let Ellen move ahead as she wished. Libby just couldn't do it. She wasn't wired that way.

Right after lunch the summons came.

"Explain this," Ellen said, slamming the report on the desk with such force that the vase with the orchid vibrated.

Libby, who had yet to sit down, shifted her gaze from the report back to Ellen, her expression cool. For a moment she and Ellen studied each other eye to eye. "I think it's self-explanatory."

"And I thought you understood that circumstances have changed over the past two years." Ellen tapped a manicured nail on the desk for emphasis.

"I agreed to consider that possibility, but after researching the matter I decided my initial recommendations are valid."

"I won't have this in the report."

Libby hooked her thumbs in the front pockets of her khakis. "I already sent a copy of my recommendations to the state manager."

Ellen's eyebrows shot up from behind her shiny glasses. "Why would you do that?"

"I wanted him to be aware of a possible conflict of interest."

"Conflict of…" Libby had touched a nerve. "If anyone has a conflict of interest, it's you."

Libby tilted her head. "How so? I'm not trying to get more grazing time for an influential person who could benefit my career."

Ellen's cheeks first paled and then went red. "Leave." It was an order. Libby obeyed.

She had no idea what would happen next. Ellen couldn't fire her, since Libby had seven excellent performance reviews in her file, but she could make Libby's professional life miserable.

Bring it on, Libby thought as she walked back to her office. At worst, Ellen would attempt to follow through with her threat to merge Libby's position with those of other regions, but Libby figured that once Ellen came to understand that the media would be involved—and the media would definitely be involved—she might back down. At best, her boss would recognize a losing battle and definitely back down. A solution somewhere in between would see Libby reprimanded and "remediated," and hopefully by the time the process was under way, Ellen would be on her way up the ladder and out of the state of Nevada.

Libby was hoping for one of the latter two options, but she was more than ready to deal with the first—having her position taken away.

"How'd it go?" Stephen asked from his desk as Libby flopped down onto her rolling chair and reached for the apple on the corner of her desk.

"About as expected," she said, biting into the fruit. "I think my relationship with our boss has suffered."

"I told you to play ball."

She gave Stephen a deadly glare. "No. I'm not having that woman gather my mustangs for no good reason."

"What if she goes over your head?"

Libby gestured with the apple. "Let her. I refuse to play this game." Stephen was obviously worried. "Hey, it'd be hard to fire me for defending a scientific position."

"But they could transfer you."

"To where? I'm already in the smallest field office in the state." She took another bite of the apple.

"Maybe out of state," Stephen said on a sigh.

MADDIE RACED OUT of Jillian's car, her ponytail bobbing as she ran, and hit Kade hard. "Dad, I missed you!"

"I missed you, too, squirt."

"Is the house ready for us?"

"Yes."

Her face fell. "I want to stay in the trailer."

Jillian maintained her smile, but Kade knew she was less than thrilled that her daughter had been staying in a horse trailer, conveniently forgetting her hantavirus fears.

"We'll be back Sunday night."

"Bye, Mom."

Jillian walked away slowly, and Kade could see it bothered her that Maddie was so happily abandoning her. "Wait here," he said to Maddie, and then he jogged over to the car. Jillian rolled down her window.

"She'll be totally ready to go when you come back."

Jillian appeared surprised that Kade was offering reassurance.

"Thanks," she said after a brief hesitation. "Have fun."

"We will."

"And if she gets on a horse…"

"She'll wear a helmet. I promise."

Kade had an excellent evening with his daughter, cooking hot dogs over the grill, listening to the many issues a nine-year-old faced as third grade ended and fourth grade loomed ahead.

She couldn't wait for her crafts class the next day, and then the 4-H meeting on Sunday. She was going to take Sugar Foot and be a guest on the trail ride. She practically vibrated with excitement.

The next day Kade took Maddie to the library as planned. He left her in the capable hands of the librarian, Allie Davis, a woman he'd known from high school, who smiled shyly at him. While Maddie was crafting, he'd be shopping and seeing about getting a few more building essentials. He figured they should both be done about the same time, and then they'd stop by the café for an ice cream.

Kira Ross, Jason's wife, had called and made arrangements to come over in a few days to discuss real estate, so Kade was feeling better about the house. He also felt slightly more positive about Jillian and the custody issue, since she'd brought Maddie down without much of a tussle. This time. The only thing truly weighing on his mind right now was Blue.

And maybe Libby.

No...*definitely* Libby.

LIBBY WENT INTO the courthouse to pay her nearly forgotten truck registration. By some miracle, while digging through the mail, she'd found the envelope stuck inside a magazine she'd yet to read, and thus she'd avoid the late fee.

She trotted up the steps, paid an outrageous price for the tiny sticker, then went to put it on the corner of her license plate.

"Hi."

Libby turned to see Kade's daughter standing behind her, and her heart rate quickened in spite of herself. Unnerved by a child. Just great. "Uh, hi."

The girl kept standing there. Watching Libby while she rubbed the dirt off the top of the old sticker with her thumb, then wiped her thumb on her jeans. Libby peeled off the backing, then pressed the sticker into place. The kid stayed put.

"Is your dad here?" She couldn't imagine Kade letting his daughter run around town by herself.

"Nope. He'll be back at two. Crafts was over a few minutes early." Maddie nodded in the direction of the library, and Libby realized the girl must have been taking a class there while Kade ran errands.

"Oh. Well…" Libby started edging toward her truck door.

"You want to see what I made?"

"Sure." Libby smiled. Kind of. The girl held up a pink-and-silver lanyard woven of plastic cord. "Cool."

Maddie beamed. "Now that I know how to make them, I'm going to make lots of them."

"Good plan."

"You're the wild-horse lady. Dad told me."

"That's me."

"Is something wrong?"

"No. Why?"

Maddie shrugged and Libby realized she was acting weird. Well, she couldn't help it. Not only was she not used to being around children, this was no ordinary kid. This was *the* kid.

"Just wondering."

"Nothing's wrong."

"Have you read *Misty of Chincoteague?*"

"Yes, I have."

"Do you have wild ponies here?"

"No, just wild horses."

"That's too bad. I like horses, but ponies are cute. What's your favorite horse book?"

"The Black Stallion."

"Dad read me that one. It was great."

Libby's mouth tightened at the thought of Kade reading *The Black Stallion* to his little girl.

"Well, I have to go," Libby said, turning, her registration receipt crumpled in her hand. "Your dad should be here soon, right?"

"Five minutes."

"Okay. See you around." Libby was ready to leave when Maddie held up the lanyard. "You can have this one."

"I, uh…" The refusal died on Libby's lips when she saw the pride in the girl's face. "Thanks." Libby took the lanyard just as Kade drove up, parking behind her truck.

"Hi, Dad," Maddie said as he got out.

"Hey, Maddie. What'd you make in crafts?"

"I gave it to her."

Libby lifted the lanyard. Kade ran his fingers over the bumpy plastic surface, and Libby tried not to notice how warm they were as they brushed her hand.

"Nice job."

"Thanks, Dad. I'm making you one, too, but first we have to buy some plastic stuff. I didn't think you'd want pink and silver."

"Any color is fine with me." Kade frowned. "Where's your backpack?"

Maddie popped a hand over her mouth. "I'll be right back." Quickly she ran up the library steps.

He turned his attention to Libby. "Thanks for watching her."

"It was more a case of her watching me," Libby said.

"Whatever. I'll have to explain to her that she needs to stay in the library until I come get her next time."

"So…is she here for a while?"

"Just this weekend, but I get more time with her in the summer and I figure she'll want to do more classes."

"Yeah. Well, I've got to go." Libby was aware that she sounded cold, or maybe a bit freaked out, but she didn't care.

"Lib?" he said. She glanced back. "Maddie's a good kid."

"Yeah, I know, Kade. But the thing is… she's not *my* kid."

And he could read anything into that he wanted.

Maddie, the kid who wasn't hers, came

running back down the steps then with her backpack in one hand. "Libby?" she called.

Libby met Kade's eyes, then forced another smile. "Yes?"

"The library lady says you have a wild horse with floppy ears."

Libby drew in a breath. "George."

"Can I see him?" Maddie glanced up at her father and then back at Libby, who felt neatly trapped.

"Sure."

"We won't have time this weekend," Kade said. "We'll figure out another time."

"For real?"

"For real."

Maddie turned hopeful eyes toward Libby. "I get to come back again next weekend because I missed my last one. Mom says. Can I see him then?"

"He's really not all that handsome," Libby said.

"I don't care. He's a mustang."

"LIBBY." STEPHEN MET her in the hall just as she left their office for a bout with the photocopy machine. He glanced at Ellen's door, then gestured for her to follow him back into the office. Once inside, he closed the door and leaned back against it. "Ellen got the okay for an emergency gather."

Libby's pulse jumped. "How?" she demanded. Especially since she, the wild horse specialist, had been totally bypassed in the process.

"She has friends in high places, I guess." Stephen's thin mouth thinned even more. "And with the new regs…well, you know."

Yes, she did. Since the federal budget was in deep trouble and it was too expensive to keep wild horses in holding areas for more than a month or two, those not immediately adoptable would be euthanized.

"The Jessup Valley?" she asked.

"I'm not entirely certain, but that's the area she's been so worked up about. And it would make Joe Barton happy."

"I don't get it. Why does she want Barton happy? He contributes to campaigns, but…" Libby gestured helplessly.

"Joe Barton is friends with the Secretary of the Interior. *Close* friends." Stephen spoke with quiet authority.

Libby's mouth fell open. She snapped it shut again.

"I don't think even you can fight this battle, Lib."

She knew the undersecretary had nothing to do with the decision to gather the horses—he wouldn't even be aware of what went on in a tiny region of Nevada—but as Ellen continued to advance professionally, having a guy like Joe Barton on her side, saying positive things to his friends in high places, could have a positive effect on her career.

Libby sat down and drummed her fingers on the arms of her chair.

"By the way, you didn't hear this from me," Stephen said.

She glanced over at him, seeing that he was concerned about being caught in the cross fire. This job was important to him, since it allowed him to live close to his parents. "Of course not."

Libby wondered how long it would take Ellen to break the happy news to her. Stephen, it turned out, only knew about the gather because Francine, the receptionist, had overheard a phone conversation early that morning before Ellen realized she was in the office. Francine had told Stephen, who'd then passed the news along to Libby and Fred.

Ellen had no idea that her entire staff was already aware of her deal, so when she took her morning stroll through the offices, she wore a serene expression. Libby did the same, although inwardly she was anything but serene.

She debated options and then dug through her correspondence file. She pulled out a distinctive pale green envelope, shaking her head as she thought about how much she had always hated getting these letters from the Run Wild Run Free Society, a group that automatically protested every mustang gather, bringing legal action whenever they were able to. Well, the group might just prove useful now.

When she went to lunch, she took the letter and her cell phone with her. Her first call was to the helicopter company that was contracted for mustang gathers. One of her regular pilots answered and told Libby that he thought something was lined up for the end of the month. They'd gotten the heads-up that morning, but she hadn't heard it from him. Libby assured him she hadn't.

Only one week away. Crap. Libby thanked the pilot and then pulled the envelope out of her back pocket. She punched in the number on the Run Wild letterhead and politely asked for her nemesis, Violet Parson.

ELLEN WAS WAITING for Libby in her office when she got back.

"Hi, Ellen," Libby said, a bit unnerved to see her boss where she hadn't expected her to be. She forced herself to sound upbeat. Had the pilot called Ellen? Libby didn't think he had, since the two of them had always had a good relationship, but anything was possible.

"I'd like a moment of your time."

"Sure." Libby's false cheerfulness was obviously irritating Ellen, but she didn't care.

"Libby, I'm sorry, but I'm afraid your position has been absorbed."

Libby stared blankly at Ellen for a moment before saying, "Absorbed—what the hell does that mean?"

Ellen drew herself up, automatically adjusting her glasses. "I don't appreciate unprofessional language in the office."

Libby shrugged. "Hey, I've been absorbed. I couldn't help myself."

Ellen set her jaw. "You'll receive an official

letter, of course, but I thought I'd tell you in person."

"So much more fun to twist the knife that way, don't you think?" Libby asked.

"That's uncalled-for," Ellen replied in a deadly tone, shaking the file she held at Libby. "I told you the budget was in trouble."

"But not in so much trouble that you can't scrape together some taxpayer money for an emergency gather."

Bright spots appeared on Ellen's cheekbones. "Where did you get that information?"

"Don't do this, Ellen. The gather is uncalled-for."

The blonde smiled icily. "What gather?"

Libby had to admit that she was impressed by Ellen's tactics. The woman could stonewall for days, denying that any kind of a gather was about to occur. Libby couldn't jeopardize Francine or the helicopter pilot by ratting them out. Not when they had done her the favor of passing along information she sorely needed.

"You'll be taking over Stephen's range-conservation duties as of next week," Ellen announced, as if it was an afterthought, when she started for the door.

"And what will Stephen be doing?"

Ellen looked back over her shoulder. "He'll be shifted to a part-time position for now."

"You're cutting his hours?" All to get back at *her?*

"We are in the midst of a serious budget crisis." Ellen stepped into the hall, her mission accomplished, then turned back again. "And if we ever do gather, I don't think we'll have the money to conduct an adoption." She smiled coldly and disappeared.

Libby took the rest of the afternoon off. She simply walked out the door. She had hours and hours of comp time coming. It was time to take it—before she got herself fired for calling her boss a bitch.

She drove back to Otto, seething. Poor Stephen. And her mustangs…

Realistically, the herd could come back from the gather, even if it was reduced by half. It would take time, but barring interference and hard winters, the numbers would rebound. It was Blue she was worried about. In order to keep the herd as healthy as possible, no old or infirm horses would be released.

Horses such as Blue would be destroyed.

CHAPTER NINE

"HEY, KADE…"

"Sheri. What's up?"

"Could you put a girl up for the night?"

Kade frowned as he took a quick survey of the trailer. It was clean enough, but pretty damned small—especially for two adults who were not sleeping together. "Sure, but… Otto isn't exactly on the road to anywhere."

"I'm driving to Salt Lake and thought I'd stop by and say hello on the way." Kade refrained from pointing out that "stopping by" entailed a four-hour detour. Obviously she wanted to see him.

"I'm staying in my horse trailer."

"I've done that before." And she had, back when they were dating. But now he didn't think she'd be very comfortable in Maddie's roomette with its plastic folding door.

"Is something wrong?"

"No." She spoke lightly, which told him something must be up, something she didn't want to discuss over the phone.

"When can I expect you?"

"Today around four?"

"So you're already on the road?"

"Yes, I am."

"Okay. See you soon."

Kade hung up, puzzled as to why Sheri would be "stopping by." It couldn't be bad news for him, since she'd already given him that. And he figured he could put any thoughts of having made the short list for the Rough Out jeans indestructibility campaign out of his head. Not that he'd had many such thoughts; sometimes in a weak moment he thought about what a nice boost to his income a few days' work, posing, would be.

Libby would laugh her ass off if she saw him being directed on how to look and how to smile while he was getting his picture taken. Move your thigh. Raise your chin, lower your eyelids. Laugh. Scowl. Smirk.

Besides, he'd been researching trade schools online at the library and had suffered major sticker shock. Education was expensive. But employment without an education was damned difficult. He still didn't know exactly what he wanted to be when he grew up, but "cowboy" wasn't cutting it.

Sheri called two hours later from Otto, and Kade gave her directions to the ranch. Upon arriving, she got out of the low-slung car, her dark hair ruffling in the breeze. Linking arms, they walked to the trailer.

"So what's happening?"

"I may have an offer for you." He stopped and turned to look down at her. She smiled. "You made the short list."

He almost wished he hadn't, because now he'd be hoping.

"You must have done some talking."

"I did," she said as they started to walk again. "And I may have made some promises on your behalf, but I'm sure you'll keep them."

"Of course I will. What promises?"

"Reliability, things like that. I found out that one of the campaign managers is a recovering alcoholic. He's the guy I approached. I mentioned that there's nothing tougher than turning your life around, and he seemed interested. He just wants to be certain that you're fully on the wagon."

He stared down at his agent, at a loss for

words for a moment. Finally he came up with, "I really appreciate this."

"And I really appreciate the percentage I'll be getting out of the deal." She smiled at him as he opened the door to the trailer, then preceded him into the tiny living quarters.

"I think this is even smaller than I remembered."

"There's a couple of motels in town. The house is ready for habitation, but...I don't sleep there."

"Why?"

"Long story." They'd dated for a couple of months, but much as he enjoyed Sheri's company he'd never been able to tell her about his dad or his childhood.

"I may consider the motel option. No offense." Sheri reached up to touch his face. She was a toucher. And they'd shared some fun times before admitting that as much as they liked each other, they wouldn't make it as a couple. The relationship had been safe, civilized and...bland. "But first, I'm hungry and I thought we should go out to eat. I'll fill you in and you can tell me about life in Otto."

"Bar or café?"

"Those are my choices?"

"Those are them."

"I'll think about it while we drive."

Sheri chose the café, which Kade assured her was wise, since it was Friday night in a town that liked to have fun. Not that Sheri wouldn't find the action at the bar entertaining, but Kade wasn't in the mood. As it was, they both enjoyed their steaks and then settled back for coffee and pie à la mode before Sheri discussed business.

Sheri thought Kade was as good as hired. All he had to do was keep his nose clean and charm the pants off everyone in an interview that she was in the process of setting up.

There'd already been two interviews before his, but the other candidates hadn't panned out—one because he was involved in a DUI incident and the other because of a messy custody battle.

Kade set his cup down. "You realize I could easily have been involved in either of those situations."

"But you weren't and you won't be. All they want is a tough, attractive veteran rodeo cowboy who hasn't gotten himself into the papers anytime lately." She made a circle with her fork. "Can you keep yourself out of trouble, or are you planning to knock over a bank or something?"

Kade smiled. "Tempting, but no. I plan to get my money the old-fashioned way. By selling my body."

"Good." Sheri took another bite of pie, half closing her eyes. "Man, this is excellent. Have you had Maddie down yet?"

"Yeah. She likes the trailer because everything is so small."

"That'll change when she gets older. She'll want a bathroom big enough to shave her legs in."

"Stop," Kade said, holding up a hand.

Sheri laughed, then her expression sobered. "I think this may be your last chance, Kade."

"I won't screw up again. I need something that'll see me through until I can get some training, nail down a decent job."

"This would be that something, Kade."

"I sure hope you're right."

THE DOOR TO Kade's house was open, as it had been the last time she'd come, so Libby walked in, rapping on the frame as she did so. It was the last place she wanted to be, but Kade needed to know what was happening with Blue. She was half-afraid of what he might do once he found out, but that wasn't her concern.

"Kade, are you here?" She glanced around the nearly empty kitchen and suppressed a shudder. The house was practically gutted, but it still had an unhappy feel to it. Hopelessness and unresolved issues. No wonder Kade didn't sleep there.

Kade stepped out into the hallway then, followed by a petite dark-haired woman. Libby's gut clenched for no reason she could think of. She should have known he had a girlfriend. He was a good-looking former celebrity.

"Libby." He seemed both surprised and embarrassed.

"Sorry to barge in," Libby said matter-of-factly, glad that they were dressed.

Kade gestured to the woman who preceded him. "This is Sheri—"

"Who's just about to leave," the woman interrupted before smiling warmly at Libby, making dimples show in her cheeks and extending a well-manicured hand. "I'm Kade's agent. Sheri Mason. We needed to talk a little business, and now I'm going to have a restful evening in one of your fine motels."

"I'm Libby Hale." She didn't know whether to allow herself to be charmed or disgusted by the fact that anyone could be so…well, charming. The woman practically twinkled.

"Nice to meet you." Sheri grabbed her purple designer purse off Kade's new countertop, then kissed him on the cheek. "I'll give you a call tomorrow and tell you what I've set up."

She gave Libby a tiny wave before sailing out the door.

"I'll be back in a sec," Kade said before disappearing into the twilight after her. Libby waited. And waited. She was at the tapping-her-toe stage when he finally returned.

Libby delivered all the bad news in one shot, before he could say anything. "They're going to gather Blue's herd," she said. "And with the new federal mandates, he'll be euthanized. Too infirm to put back out and not adoptable."

Kade's expression froze. "When will they gather?"

"Soon."

"Shit." Kade paced across the room. "Then I guess I have to go and get him."

"How will you do that?" Libby folded her arms across her chest.

"Probably cut him out of the herd. Shouldn't be too hard with him at the rear like that. Then maybe use Granddad's trap to corral him."

"And then what? You're going to load a horse that's run wild for fourteen years into a trailer and haul him away?"

"I don't know," Kade said impatiently.

Libby took a couple of paces herself, but away from him and toward the kitchen window. All she could see was a reflection of her face. *Go home, Libby. Just…go home.*

"You'll need help," she said.

He frowned. "I'll do it on my own."

"Yeah, right. That'll be a snap." She turned around, leaning against the old sink and folding her arms across her again. Shutting him out, while offering to help. That made sense.

"I can't let you risk your job. I don't think a government employee should be involved in—"

"What? Cutting an escaped domestic horse out of the herd?"

"Damn it, Lib…"

"I helped you put him out there. I'll help bring him home."

"Maddie's coming tomorrow."

That took the wind out of her sails, but she sucked it up, just as Menace had told her to. "We can bring her with us. Ride out and do some reconnaissance, make a plan." She paused, meeting his gaze solemnly. "We'll put the plan into action on Monday, after Maddie has gone home."

"Are you sure about this?"

"Can she handle the ride?"

His expression was utterly serious when he said, "I'm more concerned about you. Don't you work Monday?"

"I'm taking my comp time."

"Why are you doing this, Lib?"

She bit her lip, wondering the same thing, but knowing she had to do it. "If we get caught, I'm probably the only person around who has a legitimate reason for messing with a government herd."

"And that's it?"

"What else could there be?"

LIBBY DROVE HER own truck to the trailhead, where they had agreed to meet. Kade and

Maddie were already there, Kade on one of Joe Barton's colts and Maddie mounted on his sorrel mare, wearing a cowboy shirt and a white riding helmet. Maddie waved and, ever the good sport, Libby waved back before getting out of her truck.

Maddie was cute, but Libby had never been much of a kid person. No, she took that back. At one point in time she'd wanted about six children—all boys that looked like Kade. She wasn't wanting that so much anymore.

Maddie gave a delighted laugh when Libby unloaded George, the floppy-eared mustang.

"How'd his ears get like that?" Maddie asked as George turned his head toward her and stuck his nose out for a pat. Maddie stroked his muzzle from atop her horse.

"Mutation."

"He was born that way," Kade added as Maddie wrinkled her forehead.

"He looks like my teacher's rabbit, Flopsy. How'd you get him?"

"I adopted him," Libby said as she checked the cinch.

Maddie's eyes widened and she shot a hopeful glance at her father. "No," he replied before she could say a word. "We are not adopting a mustang."

"But, Dad…"

Libby focused on bridling George as she also tried to deal with weirdly conflicting emotions. She actually liked Kade's daughter, but hated what she represented. It was not going to be an easy day.

They set off down the road, Maddie happily talking about horses and Libby thinking she couldn't believe she was riding with Kade and his daughter. Had anyone told her ten years ago, when she felt as if her heart had been ripped from her chest, that she'd be on an outing with Kade and his child, she would have bet twenty million dollars it would never happen. Ever.

And yet here she was.

Maddie turned out to be a decent rider. She handled the mare with confidence, and her seat was excellent. In fact, she was fairly strict with the mare, putting up with no nonsense, such as eating along the trail, which caused Libby to smile more than once. Maddie had inherited her father's ability with horses.

It took an hour to reach the mustang trap. They could have driven to it on the rutted mountain road, but Libby and Kade had agreed it would be better to make it an incidental stop on a pleasure ride so Maddie wouldn't be aware that the trap was the destination. The girl was sharp, and every now and then she unnerved Libby by looking from Kade to Libby and back again, her expression thoughtful.

Don't even think about it, kid.

It seemed that Maddie wanted both her parents to be living happily ever after—which Kade was free to do as soon as he found someone who wasn't afraid to take a chance on him. Maybe Sheri the agent was that person.

Maybe Libby hated that idea.

Maybe Libby was being controlled by her hormones and emotions, instead of her perfectly capable brain.

As they approached the mustang trap, Libby was impressed by the shape it was in. She hadn't seen the trap in years, not since she and Kade had ridden up to see it as teenagers. Kade's grandfather had used wire, brush and juniper posts to make two fences that formed a long semiparallel funnel leading into a concealed corral. When they'd visited years ago, some of the wire could still be seen, but now the entire structure was overgrown with sagebrush, making natural-looking banks of vegetation on either side of the trail leading in. The barriers were almost thirty feet apart at the beginning of the funnel, and as one traveled farther inside, the sides began to close in. Finally there was a sharp L turn leading directly into the catch pen.

"What is this, Dad?"

"Just a fence," Kade said.

Even the gate was in decent shape.

Now all Kade had to do was ambush Blue at the proper moment and run him into the trap.

Then load him into the trailer.

And finally take him home and get him healthy. Without getting caught. Like Libby had said earlier, it should be a snap.

THEY CAMPED OUT that night, and Maddie was quite disgusted that they did not sleep under the stars with ropes around their sleeping bags. Kade had a hard time convincing her that scorpions didn't care about ropes, but finally she agreed to sleep in the truck. After Maddie went to bed, Kade and Libby sat side by side in folding chairs, under the pretense of watching the stars. But truth be told, they were both too keyed up to sleep.

Libby knew the signs in Kade; she was certain he remembered them in her. They'd practically been a married couple. So why had she been so afraid of getting married back then, making their relationship permanent and legal?

Because they'd had no life skills.

She'd been afraid of ruining a good thing by not knowing how to be married. It seemed laughable now, but back then, with virtually no support system since her parents were such drunks, it hadn't seemed so laughable. It had seemed sensible. Later, after discovering exactly how monogamous Kade was, her thinking seemed inspired.

But sometimes she wondered what would have happened if she hadn't wanted more time to grow up.

"Why are you here?" Kade asked, breaking the silence.

"I told you. I helped let Blue go. I want to help bring him home."

"And that's it." He didn't fully believe her, probably because it wasn't the entire truth.

Libby kept her eyes on the sky. "I'm having trouble at work with my boss, too. That's why they're gathering without me. I'm a range con again."

Kade shifted in his chair. "They took your job?"

"*Absorbed* it."

"What the hell does that mean?"

She smiled without looking his way. "That was *my* question. Anyway, it's gone. For now. I'm not finished by any means, but…well, I thought it'd be best to get this over with before I start the battle."

She looked at him then, barely able to make out his features, but she could see his teeth when he smiled. "You're here for revenge?"

"I'm here for a horse," she said. "Now I have a question."

"What?"

"If you're putting your place on the market, where will you keep a stud?"

"I'm going to try to buy a smaller property near Elko, so I can live close to Maddie.

There's some smaller horse properties in the area."

"Will you geld him?"

"I've been thinking about that. I'd kind of like a couple of colts out of him."

"I wouldn't mind one myself," Libby said just as a light flashed across the sky.

"Shooting star," Kade murmured. They'd wished on hundreds of them during the summer meteor showers when they were kids.

"Meteor burning up in the atmosphere."

"You used to be more romantic."

"I wonder what happened."

"*I* happened," he said matter-of-factly.

"Yeah, you did. I don't think I've been romantic since."

"I heard you were dating the vet from Wesley."

"Yes."

"Is it serious?"

"None of your business."

He leaned closer. His forearm was on the armrest of her chair and she could feel his warmth. She didn't know if he would kiss her with his daughter so close, but she got her answer seconds later when he cupped the base of her neck, his fingers splaying over the back of her head, and pulled her lips to his, meeting them softly.

Libby stilled. Their breaths mingled for a taut moment and then Kade lightly kissed her again, touching her top lip with the tip of his tongue. Tracing it before he covered her mouth again. Tasting her. Testing her. Libby shuddered and pulled away. Otherwise she might have pushed him out of the chair and onto his back and had her way with him, scorpions be damned.

Her body had not forgotten Kade. Her body longed for him.

This was not good. She got to her feet, snapped the chair shut and leaned it against the side of the truck.

"I'm going to bed." She'd rolled her sleeping bag out in the bed of the truck—Kade had volunteered to sleep in the dustier nose of the horse trailer. After she'd wormed her way into her sleeping bag, fully dressed, Libby lay still, waiting to hear the trailer door shut before her muscles finally let go and she allowed herself to relax.

Oh, yeah. Kade still had the power to move her. This was not good at all.

THE NEXT MORNING they rode to the ridge top and watched the mustangs migrate up the trail from the valley to the high country, where they would graze until it was time to come down to water. They were so distant they were little more than dots, but Maddie was still excited. When Maddie asked if Blue was there, Kade told her they were too far away to tell—but Blue was there, a solitary dot trailing the herd.

They parted company at the trailhead around noon, Libby loading George in her trailer and driving away, while Kade unsaddled his two horses and answered about a thousand questions about the desert and wild horses. Before they left, Maddie saw a horny toad and Kade scooped it up.

"You can't catch just any lizard, because some bite, but you can catch these."

"Can I keep it?" Maddie asked, her eyes wide.

"He'll die unless you get a hot stone for him to sit on to digest his food. And don't you think he's happier out here in the dirt, chasing ants?"

"Yeah, I guess." Maddie stroked the tiny toad with one finger, grinning as the animal squatted lower with each light stroke.

"Am I raising a desert rat?"

"I think so," Maddie said as she gently took the toad from Kade, then bent down to let it scuttle off her hand into the silty soil. "Just like you. Right?"

Kade looked down at his daughter with her lopsided blond ponytail and the smudge of dust across her face and smiled. And he was really glad Jillian hadn't heard this particular conversation. Maddie might be a ballerina who was learning to ride English, but she was also a tough little tomboy who played softball.

"I like Libby," Maddie said out of the blue as they were driving home. "She was kind of scary at first, though."

She's afraid of you. And Kade wasn't sure what to do about it. Wasn't much he *could* do about it. "Sometimes people act scary when they're around things they're not used to."

"Like kids."

"Exactly." Kade reached out to gently tug her ponytail. "I can't think of anything scarier than a kid."

CHAPTER TEN

THE MOON WAS STILL bright when Kade pulled into Libby's driveway early Monday morning, his father's beat-up trailer hitched to his truck. Stock panels hung on the side of the trailer and camping gear was stashed in the back of the truck. Libby didn't plan to spend the night, but this was not a cut-and-dried mission. Anything was possible. Including arrest.

Libby led her saddled mare to the trailer and loaded her, tying her next to Sugar Foot.

"Last chance to change your mind," Kade said before he shut the trailer door.

"As if." Libby was rather enjoying secretly thumbing her nose at Ellen. Immature? Yes. Satisfying? You bet. She opened the passenger-side door and climbed into the truck, which still had a faint odor of perfume clinging to the upholstery.

"Where does your girlfriend live?" she asked casually as Kade put the truck into Drive.

"Boise. And she's my agent."

"Your agent." Odd concept to Libby, Kade having an agent. "I see."

"We did date for a while after I got divorced."

"You appear to have had an amicable parting."

"I've learned a lot about conducting relationships," Kade said before turning the key in the ignition.

"You had nowhere to go but up."

Kade pulled out of the driveway onto the county road. Libby settled back in her seat, watching the ranch lights as they started coming on, thinking how strange this situation was. They'd been best friends when they'd first set out to release Blue. Now they were... what?

They were exes. Ex-best friends. Ex-lovers. Off to reverse their mission, to try to save the same horse they'd saved before. Only this time a different kind of tension hung in the air.

Libby was not afraid of getting caught, but

she was afraid of the strong draw she still felt toward Kade. Which was why she kept staring straight ahead, studying lights that did not interest her in the least. "So was Sheri just visiting?" she finally asked.

"She, uh, might have gotten me a job. I'm interviewing with Rough Out in a few days." He sounded self-conscious.

Libby raised her eyebrows. "You'll be beefcaking again?"

Kade smiled. "I hope. For a while, anyway. I need the income. It may take some time to sell the ranch, and I've got to pay for job training meanwhile."

"For what kind of job?"

"That's the big question."

The sun topped the hills as they turned onto the Jessup Valley road. There were tire tracks visible from a truck and trailer, and Libby glanced over at Kade. She really hoped no one was in this canyon. It would screw up their plans royally.

He said nothing.

They drove along the narrow hunting road the mustangs traveled on their way to water. Deep gray clouds were gathering to the south, which surprised Libby. Over the past two years they'd had rampant thunderstorms, most of them dry, all lightning and no rain, but so far this spring there'd been none. Until today. She hoped they wouldn't be dealing with lightning. Or fire.

When they reached the spur leading to the old mustang trap, Kade stopped the truck and they got out. Libby went back to unload Mouse. She tightened the cinch, then ran a hand over the mare's neck, waiting for her to relax her belly so she could tighten just a little more, since they'd be riding up and down mountain trails.

"Lib."

She looked up to find Kade nearer than she'd expected. "What?" She had to make herself hold her ground. She was torn between stepping closer and walking around to the other side of the horse.

"Are you *sure* you want to get involved in this? I know you're downplaying what might happen to you if we get caught."

"This is the right thing to do. We let him go. Besides, you deserve to have Blue. Have the time you didn't get with him because of your dad."

"All right." But he didn't move away.

Libby went back to checking her cinch, doing her best to keep her movements natural, instead of jerky. She hadn't come up here to feel edgy about Kade. She'd come up here to rescue a horse.

KADE DREW IN A breath and stepped back, away from Libby, away from temptation. It killed him that after all this time he still wanted her so much it hurt, and she wasn't about to let it happen. Once bitten, twice shy. With Libby it was more like twenty times shy. He knew she had her reasons, knew he and their small group of friends had been her only support system while they'd been growing up. She'd been closest to him in every possible way, and he'd been the one who'd betrayed her trust. Libby wouldn't give him another chance to do the same thing again.

She gathered the reins and put her foot into the stirrup, mounting quickly. Kade did likewise and started off down the trail. He wanted to go first, so that he wouldn't be spending his time staring at her.

They'd briefly discussed their plan on the drive to the spur. Now he just hoped it worked. If they couldn't get Blue this time, it would be too late to try again. Libby had called her office mate, Stephen somebody, and gotten word that the gather was on—planned for the end of the week, before anyone had time to do anything about it. Libby was still grumbling about how Ellen should never have been able to get the gather pushed through so fast. But the word *emergency* held a lot of power, and apparently this was considered an emergency gather.

Kade wondered just whose emergency this was—the horses' or Joe Barton's?

Employer or not, and for all the good it would probably do, Kade planned to talk to Joe when he got back. The guy was motivated by money and success. Kade needed the job—especially if Rough Out didn't come through—but he had his principles. There was room on the range for cattle *and* mustangs, if Joe didn't let himself get greedy.

So how did a guy go about discussing greed with his boss?

It should make for an interesting conversation.

LIBBY WATCHED KADE'S back as they rode single file up the trail, and she wondered how this was going to play out. She'd made a few more phone calls the evening before to the saner groups who protested horse gathers. E-mails would have been easier, but they were also more traceable. She was doing the right thing, but evidence of that in the hands of a bureaucrat who wanted to get rid of her could be dangerous. Amazing how words and intent could be twisted by a master. But she and Violet, the head of Run Wild Run Free, were developing a grudging mutual respect, which would help Libby's job go more smoothly if she ever got "unabsorbed."

They stopped in a high spot in the foothills, where they could watch the trail but still be far enough away so that their horses wouldn't call out to the herd, warning the mustangs. And then they waited. And waited. Silently. They could have talked, since they were far enough away, but they didn't. Instead, they watched the valley below, each lost in their own thoughts.

It was close to noon when they spotted the herd moving down the narrow road. Kade nodded at Libby, then started cross-country on Sugar Foot, heading into the gulley that separated them from the bench—a low, flat-topped ridge—paralleling the road.

Libby turned Mouse and followed Kade. They worked their way into the gulley and up the other side of the bench, then Libby stopped and Kade rode forward slowly, up to where he could just see the herd. He stayed still for several minutes, then waved for Libby to follow him. The plan was to wait until the main part of the herd passed and then cut off the end horse—Blue. Libby had total faith in Kade's timing. He had his faults, but he was damned talented at herd work.

They crested the bench, coming at the end of the herd at an angle, spooking the leaders and turning back the horses that lagged at the rear—two mares with foals at their sides, and Blue.

The small band reversed course, cantering up the road they'd just walked down, tails up, heads held high. Libby urged Mouse to go faster, glad she was on a sure-footed mustang as they raced over the rough ground before cutting between the bay mare and Blue, edging the mare and foal off to the side, allowing them to return to the main herd while pushing Blue on up the road. Kade did the same, turning back the other mare, then charged up ahead, past Blue, who was starting to labor due to his bad leg. He pulled Sugar Foot up and then rolled back, effectively cutting off Blue's escape route. The roan whirled, despite his injury, and tried to outmaneuver Kade's mare, but Libby urged Mouse forward, cutting off the new escape route.

The stud turned to the right, into the funnel. Libby followed Kade and Blue into the opening.

Kade vaulted off his horse as soon as Blue turned the L-shaped corner and entered the trap, heaving the wired-up gate across the opening. Blue panicked then, racing around the perimeter of the pen, his head high, eyes rolling. Kade wired the gate to the juniper posts on either side, then stood back and watched the horse run.

"I hope he doesn't try to go through the side," Libby said as she dismounted. She didn't know if the old fencing would hold him.

"He won't." In fact, the stud was already slowing, bobbing his head warily as he surveyed his situation. He slid to a stop in the center of the corral, snorted and then stood, his flanks heaving, his nostrils flared and showing red.

"He's changed a bit," Libby said, remembering the docile quarter horse they'd released all those years ago.

"He'll come round."

Libby wanted to ask, "When?" But instead, she said, "Now what?"

"I guess we get the trailer." Kade held out the keys. "If you don't mind."

"Not at all." Libby glanced up at the darkening sky. "It's going to rain."

"Tell me something I don't know."

"So we're going to try to load a wild stallion in the rain."

"Yeah," Kade replied, "we are." He turned to glance down at her and Libby smiled. She couldn't help it, he looked so satisfied with himself and the situation. Just as he had when he'd been sixteen.

"Anybody could catch a lame horse," she muttered as she mounted Mouse again.

"But not with such flair," Kade said.

"Stay out of that corral until I get back. My CPR card is expired."

"All right, Ma."

Libby snorted and turned Mouse toward the entrance to the trap.

It took Libby almost thirty minutes to get back to the truck, load Mouse and then drive up the narrow road to the trap. She was quite capable of backing a trailer into tight spots, but she didn't attempt the last eighth of a mile into the spur and around the corner. She'd let Kade put it where he wanted it.

She turned the truck off and walked. Rain started to fall as she rounded the corner. She hoped it was only a quick shower, but the sky was steel gray and the clouds hugged the mountaintops. She turned back to the truck and quickly stowed Kade's camp gear in the tack room of the old trailer. Then she started walking again toward the L-shaped turn, wondering what she would find on the other side.

The Kade she'd grown up with would have been over the fence, working the stud, as soon as she was out of sight on her mission to get the truck. This new Kade was waiting for her on the correct side of the fence—the one she'd left him on. And then she noticed that one entire side of him was covered with dirt and stickers.

Okay. Maybe he hadn't changed all that much.

"Any troubles?" Kade asked. He followed her gaze to his dirty clothing and gave a half smile. "Not what you think. I tripped." He pointed at a rock jutting out of the ground close to the gate.

"And now you're going to do fancy footwork with a stud? That makes me feel confident." Libby held out the keys. "I'll let you do the tricky backing with the trailer, since it's your rig."

"Fine. Keep an eye on him."

"What am I supposed to do if he decides to leave?" Libby called after Kade. He turned and flashed his old smile at her.

"You'll think of something."

It didn't take long for him to back the trailer almost as far as it would go into the funnel, just around the corner from the gate. When he reappeared, he was carrying his rope. The show was about to begin.

The rain kept coming, pattering lightly, filling the air with the pungent odor of fresh sage but not yet falling hard enough to make the ground slick. Libby glanced at the sky again. There was a patch of blue sky to the south, so it was possible they'd get a break. She didn't want either man or horse to slip and go down.

Kade went to the gate and climbed over it. Blue backed up, and then when Kade got close to the center the horse started racing around the pen again, his head bobbing each time his bad hind leg hit the ground.

"Remember me?" Kade murmured as the horse cantered past him. "I'm the guy who saved you a lot of pain."

He continued to stand in the middle of the pen, the rope in one hand, waiting for the horse to slow, which he eventually did. And the entire time Kade continued to talk.

Blue's ears would flick every now and again, making Libby wonder if, when the terror passed, the horse might remember the sound of human voices. Well and good, if he remembered Kade's. Not so good, if he remembered Kade's father's voice instead.

The rain let up and the makeshift pen grew dusty again as Kade continued to let the horse circle. When he slowed, Kade stepped back and the horse stopped.

Round-pen work had been fairly new when Kade had first gotten Blue, but they'd played with it, watching a John Lyons video that they'd checked out of the county library. Blue had been responsive then, but the big question was, would he be responsive now? They were fighting time. Fighting the potential for bad weather.

Kade got the horse moving again, then after a few circles, allowed him to stop. The horse stared at Kade for a long time, facing him, considering.

Did he remember?

Kade took a step forward, holding out his hand for the stud to smell. Another step. Blue turned his head away and moved again. But he stopped after another few steps and turned his head back toward Kade, who'd retreated to the center of the pen.

The horse took a curious step forward when Kade didn't move. Then another step. Kade moved backward. The horse followed.

And then he chewed—a sure sign that he was relaxing.

Libby let out a breath.

The horse continued to stand and regard Kade from several feet away. Kade backed up again.

And so it went until finally the stud let

Kade touch him with the coils of the rope. That was as far as Kade went. The rain started to come down for real then, and they were losing light.

"We'll have to wait until daylight to load him."

"If we wait until morning and it keeps raining, we may not get out of here." The bottom fell out of the desert when it rained, making it impossible to drive without getting stuck.

"I can't load a frightened horse in the mud, in the dark."

"I know." Libby pushed wet curls back from her forehead.

"And why aren't you wearing a hat?" Kade asked gruffly.

"Gee, *Ma,* I guess I forgot it."

He reached into his inside coat pocket and came up with a stocking hat, which he pulled down over her hair.

"There," he said as he stepped back. Libby scowled at him and he started laughing. "You look…good."

"Thanks." She reached up to tuck her hair under the edge of the hat. She'd lived in this country long enough to know it could snow in June and then be in the nineties the following week. It had been dumb to come without a warm hat. "We should get out of the rain," she said.

They unsaddled the horses and loaded them in the trailer, instead of hobbling them, so they wouldn't bother Blue, who was now pacing the pen, screaming.

Kade rolled out his bedroll on the makeshift bunk formed by the overhang of the gooseneck and they climbed up on it to sit on the padded canvas. He opened his day pack and pulled out a jar of Cheez Whiz, a packet of crackers and a couple of cans of Bud Light.

"You sure know how to feed your crew," Libby said as she picked up the jar of cheese.

"I thought we'd be in a position to cook." He handed Libby a beer. A moment later he raised his own can in a salute. "To a day's work well-done."

Libby nodded, drank and then wiped her fingers over her lips. "It's tomorrow that concerns me."

"Let's just assume it'll go well."

"You are an optimist."

"Gotta be, Lib. Otherwise I'd be in the nuthouse by now."

Libby had nothing to say to that.

They'd left the door open so they could have some light, and they watched the rain drizzling down as they ate their makeshift meal.

"Just like old times," Kade said after they'd finished the cheese and Libby grew still. "Is that so bad?"

"Let's not talk about old times. Okay?"

Kade didn't answer. He compressed his lips and continued to stare at the rain.

The silence grew heavy, interrupted only by the stallion's occasional screams, so finally Libby asked a question she'd been wondering about. "Did...your daughter ever get a chance to meet your dad?"

Kade shook his head. "I wouldn't let him meet her. When he tried to beat me up that last time, that was it. No more. And it might be rotten of me, but one of the things I liked best about being a world champion was that it showed the old man that I wasn't the loser he always told me I was."

"He must have really hated himself," Libby said softly. Kade looked at her in surprise.

"He hated me."

Libby shook her head. "You were just an easy target for his rage."

Kade eased back onto his elbows. "I guess logically that may be so, but I don't know that I can ever believe it."

"You need to have a long talk with your inner child."

"No. I need to build a future, not wallow in the past."

"You're right. I'm sorry." Libby started to slide down off the bunk, ready to go to the truck, where she'd rolled out her own sleeping bag. But Kade took hold of her arm, stopping her.

"Lib…"

She shook her head again. "No, Kade."

Kade put a rough forefinger on her bottom lip, lightly tracing it. She could barely see his expression in the dim light, but she could tell that he was frowning. Intently. She swallowed.

She was strong. She could deal with the situation. What if she didn't put a stop to what he was doing? What if she decided to see what happened? Out of curiosity, if nothing else. It wasn't as if she'd self-destruct.

Kade's palm smoothed over her cheek and then traveled around to the back of her neck, where his fingers flexed, working the tense muscles there. Libby dropped her chin, let him do his magic. It felt good. A moment later he tipped her chin up and stared at her in the twilight. The rain continued to patter on the metal roof only inches above their heads, but Libby was more aware of the sound of Kade's breathing.

What would it feel like to make love to him again? Maybe she'd allowed this lingering attraction she felt for him to grow larger and more threatening in her mind than it was in reality.

Maybe if she slept with him, she'd find out she'd been worrying about a heck of a lot of nothing.

Was it possible?

Heaven help her, she wanted to find out. And Kade, who could still read her, was well aware of her desire.

He took her face in his hands, leaned down and kissed her. Hard. No more gentle exploration. This was a man hungry for a woman. He pulled her on top of him as he eased onto his back, never losing contact with her mouth, his hands moving over the thick layers of her coat and jeans.

Libby pressed closer, the plan to get him out of her system with a heavy dose of reality growing stronger as his tongue plunged deeper into her mouth. She took hold of his hair, then lifted her chin as his lips traveled down her neck.

He eased her away then and let out a long breath, still cradling the sides of her face.

He started to say something, but Libby stopped him by pulling his mouth back to hers and kissing him deeply. He groaned and she believed he'd gotten her message. *Don't talk. Just do this and see what happens.*

She pushed his coat off his shoulders, effectively trapping his arms before she started undoing buttons, one after another, until she could open his shirt and run her palms over the muscles she had once known so well.

She stopped as her hands encountered a narrow raised ridge that crossed his abdomen. A scar that hadn't been there before. She traced it with her tongue, tasting salt. And Kade. He sucked air in through his teeth and she licked lower, past the scar to the waistband of his jeans. He struggled against the confines of the coat until he finally pulled his arms free and tossed the garment off the edge of the overhang onto the saddles below.

After that clothes started raining down from the bunk onto the floor of the tack room—shirts, jeans, underwear. Some of the clothes never made it over the edge. Libby winced as she rolled onto his belt buckle, then forgot everything as his mouth moved over her breasts, hot and wet, making her gasp.

Things hadn't changed between them. She knew him, knew what to do to make him crazy, and he returned the favor. His touch was familiar, welcome, as his fingers smoothed over her abdomen, caressing her thighs before finally pushing deeply into her. She arched against his palm, almost coming right there.

His penis was pressed hard against her leg, larger than she'd remembered. She wanted him badly—so badly that she was beginning to wonder if this plan to get him out of her system wasn't going to work out as anticipated. But she wasn't stopping.

"Do you have condoms?" she managed to ask during a brief moment of sanity.

"Everywhere." He pulled his jeans out from under her and fumbled for the wallet. "I've never taken another chance."

Moments later, before she could fully process his words, he was deep inside her, making her realize that all the memories she'd convinced herself she'd embellished over the years had indeed been true. Kade was good.

She came before she wanted to, clutching him tightly as her body throbbed. He followed not long after, collapsing against her, his skin covered with a light sheen of perspiration.

Eventually he let out a long breath, then pressed his lips to her neck. Her arms automatically tightened around him, her hands splaying over the hard muscles of his shoulders.

She could feel herself falling right back in love with him.

She wouldn't let it happen. This was a one-time shot.

Kade raised his head. "Lib?" he asked softly, running the tips of his fingers lightly down the side of her face.

She didn't know what he wanted. Reassurance? A declaration of love? "Please don't say anything."

"Don't back off, Libby."

"I have to. I have to think." She eased away from him, climbed off the bunk, leaving his warmth and searching in the darkness for her clothing. Kade pulled the string of the battery-powered light above the door. She wished he hadn't. She didn't want to see his concerned expression, didn't want to see him looking as if he was falling back in love with her, too.

After that it didn't take her long to dress. She actually managed to say good-night in a fairly normal voice, and then walked through the mud to the truck, where she slid out of her boots and climbed into her cold sleeping bag. It was too early to sleep, so there she lay, listening to Blue scream for his herd—the herd that no longer wanted him.

CHAPTER ELEVEN

IT WAS A DAMP, GRAY morning, which perfectly suited Libby's mood, but the rain had stopped and the clouds were high. Once the sun came out, the land would dry quickly. In the meantime, however, it was damned muddy.

Libby was sitting on the tailgate of the truck trying to clean the caked-on gunk off her boots with a stick when Kade opened the trailer door and stepped out, buttoning his shirt as he did so. He looked very much like a guy who'd spent the night making love, rumpled and sexy, ready for more.

"Morning," he said in a husky voice before disappearing around the corner of the trailer.

Libby bit her lip. The morning after. The reason the evening before was sometimes a bad idea. Her reality-check plan hadn't worked out at all, because the reality had proved to be even better than the memory.

Kade was gone for several minutes. She heard him talking to Blue, who'd settled during the night, and then he came back around the trailer.

"How're you doing?" he asked.

Libby glanced up at him. "I'm fine. And—" she flicked off a thick chunk of mud "—I'm glad it happened."

His expression shifted toward cautious optimism. "You are?"

"We needed it." She continued to wipe the mud off the sides of her boots.

"We needed it," he echoed in a stony voice.

She scraped away another clump of mud. "Wouldn't you say?" she asked politely, shooting him a quick look. "It…took the edge off."

"Damn it, Lib!" He stalked toward the corral. Libby watched him go, then shook her head.

They *had* needed it. And she wouldn't let it be any more than that. For once in her life she was in control of her feelings for Kade. He rocked her world, no doubt about that. She was attracted to him. She might even let herself fall back in love with him—if that hadn't already happened. But she couldn't silence the doubts. And part of her was still damned mad about what he'd done all those years ago, still wanted to punish him for the past.

Right or wrong, she couldn't help it, and that was no way to venture into a relationship.

KADE BARELY SPOKE to Libby that morning. There didn't seem to be a hell of a lot to say, other than goodbye, which was what she'd in essence told him. Kade had experienced some long nights in his checkered past, and the one he'd just been through rated right up there with the best of them, because for a while there he'd actually been hopeful. And afraid. Now she'd made the situation clear. He couldn't hang on to her. He needed to accept it and move forward.

Good thing he had the horse to focus on. He needed *some*thing.

He wouldn't say that Blue remembered him, but the horse's early training was starting to kick in. He responded to Kade's cues as he was supposed to, although Kade imagined the stud had no idea why he was behaving this way. Kade had opened the gate so that the only escape from the catch pen was into the trailer.

A few turns around the trap, then Kade let the horse rest by the trailer. A few more turns. Rest by the trailer. And that alfalfa inside looked pretty good. Blue had already had a small amount the night before, and now he wanted more. And since he'd been in a trailer before, in fact, this very trailer, dozens of times when he'd been young, it wasn't all that scary. He kept leaning farther and farther inside when Kade allowed him to stop.

Eventually he simply jumped in and Kade closed the door.

"He remembered," Libby said. She'd stood near the gate during the entire session, watching without saying a word.

"Yeah." Kade was still pissed off, with Libby, with himself.

We needed that. He needed more than *that.* He'd slept with enough buckle bunnies to know that it might scratch the itch, but in the long run it was an empty way to live life. He needed some emotional involvement, and last night he'd talked himself into believing that maybe, once she had some time to consider, Libby would see that they did have a connection. A deep one. If they hadn't, the sex wouldn't have been so spectacular.

"Think we'll get out of here?"

No. The mud was deep.

But they did get out. Kade geared down low and took it slow, keeping out of the ruts as much as possible. Blue rode like a trouper, the movement of the trailer lulling him.

"Take him to my place," Libby said when they finally pulled out of Jessup Canyon and onto the main road.

"Why?" It wasn't because she wanted to see more of him.

"He'll blend better. You have one horse and your corrals can be seen from the road. I have a dozen horses and a long driveway. Plus my corral is more suited to a stud."

He had to agree with her logic, even if he didn't want to leave his horse with her. When they reached her ranch, he backed the trailer to the pole corral, then climbed out to open the gate on one side and the trailer door on the other, making an alleyway.

Blue shoved his way out of the trailer as soon as the door opened, almost knocking Kade over. He limped into the corral, screaming. Libby's entire herd came running. *New guy on the property. Check him out.*

"Definitely less noticeable here," Libby said dryly. She glanced sideways at Kade.

For a moment they just stared at each other, then Kade looked away, back at his horse.

"He'll settle," Kade said. "And I'll see what I can do about building a stud corral on the far side of my barn."

He didn't regret retrieving Blue, but he did regret what had happened between him and Libby, since it hammered home so clearly the fact that she was not going to let him get close. She'd have sex with him, but she wouldn't let herself trust him or care about him.

Let her go, man.

"I have to fly to Las Vegas from Elko for the Rough Out interview tomorrow."

"Don't worry about anything."

Yeah. "I want to spend the night in Elko, see Maddie, but if you foresee any problems…"

"None."

"Right." He stepped back from the fence. "I'll come over and feed him."

"If you want, but it's no big deal."

"Thanks, Lib." He headed for his truck then, not caring that he'd sounded a whole lot less than grateful.

BLUE WAS STILL SCREAMING on and off when Kade drove down the driveway. Libby went out at one point and fed him again. Too much hay was bad for horses who had lived on sparse range land for so long, so she mixed in some straw to give him something to chew on, something to do.

But as far as Blue was concerned, he *had* something to do. He had a new herd, without another stud in sight, and he needed to take control.

"Get over it, big boy," Libby said as she leaned on the railings. "They aren't impressed." And indeed, her girls weren't, since none of them was in season at the moment. Things would get a lot noisier once they were. It seemed like a good time to put her herd out on the back forty, out of sight of Blue. She'd leave him George for company. Two misfit males together.

KADE HAD NEVER done well with the suit-and-tie crowd, but before, he'd met with ad execs because they wanted him. Now the situation was reversed. He was the one who needed them.

He hated it. Men in suits could smell desperation and he was doing his best to act as he always had—confident.

Confident. Who was he trying to kid? He'd been cocky. A twenty-six-year-old with a couple of world titles tended to be that way. And the execs had loved it because that cockiness seemed to say, "Hey, you, too, can have the world by the tail if you put your ass in these jeans."

Unfortunately, because of that cockiness, he'd learned one of the hardest lessons of his professional life. And that lesson was, *Everyone is replaceable.* He'd certainly been replaceable. Jillian had replaced him. Rough Out had replaced him. Only Maddie kept him number one in her heart, although Mike ran a close second.

Libby…well, she'd made it clear that she'd replaced him—with nothing. She was happy without him and hadn't needed to bring anyone else in to take his place. She was dating Sam the vet, but according to the woman at the post office, it wasn't serious.

"Mr. Danning?" The receptionist smiled warmly. "I'll escort you to the conference room."

Kade got to his feet, his best felt hat in his hands. *Escort away...*

The meeting was amazingly brief. They wanted him. Alan Prescott, the man Sheri had told him about, the recovering alcoholic, laid out the rules. As long as they were using his image, he was to live up to Rough Out standards. No substance abuse. No scandal. Nothing to make them regret taking a second chance on him, after the last sorry parting. If he was even late, there would be repercussions.

Oh, and there would be a magazine article to kick off the campaign. When they discovered that he was rebuilding his dad's place, they were excited. Perfect. Cowboy rebuilding a ranch from the ground up. Wearing Rough Out jeans. Kade had a feeling he'd be doing a lot of building with his shirt unbuttoned or all the way off. They wanted him back in Las Vegas in a matter of days for a preliminary shoot, and then they wouldn't need him again for at least a month.

With a tentative timeline that included

shooting the magazine spread at the ranch in July and the promise of contracts to sign soon, Kade left the interview and went straight to the airport. He called Sheri as he waited for his flight, told her he'd behaved himself and that she could expect contracts.

The flight was bumpy. Kade didn't care. He had income for a while and he could use it to learn a trade other than bucking or posing. Something steady. He'd never had that in his entire life and it was high time he did.

KADE CALLED JILLIAN shortly after landing to tell her he'd arrived in town and would pick up Maddie later that evening. Even if all they did was hang out at the motel swimming pool or go for pizza and a movie, he'd have some time with her.

"And I was wondering…would you be able to meet me first? Maybe grab a bite in an hour or so?" He'd had a lot of time to think that day as he'd waited for flights. And he'd also had a lot of time to think the day before, when he and Libby had driven home from Jessup Canyon in rigid silence.

"I pick Maddie up at five, which doesn't

leave a lot of time," she said, a note of bewilderment in her voice.

Dance. Or was it softball? "I'd like to talk," Kade said. *Face-to-face.* "You can bring the twins if you want."

Jillian laughed. "If I brought the twins, there'd be no talking. Which raises the question—what do you want to talk about?"

Kade drew a breath, ready to do this over the phone if that was his only option. "Me. I want to talk about me."

"Meet me at the Hacienda," Jillian said. "In twenty minutes?"

"That sounds good. And…thanks."

The Hacienda had been redecorated since the last time Kade had eaten there. The classic Mexican motif—burros and sombreros—had been replaced with bright paintings, funky furniture and blown-glass chili peppers, and the old crowd had been replaced by a newer, younger crowd. The happy hour people were already beginning to fill the place when Kade arrived, but he managed to find a table for two against the back wall.

Jillian was five minutes late, but she was the mother of twins, after all, and Kade imagined that much of her life was spent being five minutes late. She looked good, though, somehow managing to make busy-mom clothes—khakis and a light blue button-front shirt—appear stylish.

"So what do you need, Kade?" she asked as she took a seat on the opposite side of the table.

"I'm going back to work for Rough Out."

"Congratulations." She smiled distantly, and he could see that she was waiting to hear how that affected her. And Maddie.

"You mean that?" Kade asked, cocking his head slightly.

She considered the question for a moment, then her expression unexpectedly warmed. "Yes. I guess I do. You've had a rough go lately."

A waiter approached and Jillian shook her head as he held out a menu. "Just some hot tea." Kade was famished, but he ordered the same, figuring he'd eat once she left to pick up Maddie.

"Why else are we here?" Jillian asked, folding her hands on the bright yellow table-cloth. Her nails were neatly manicured as always.

"Two reasons."

She tilted her head. "Maddie."

He nodded.

"And…?" she prompted.

"Our time together, Jillie." He ran his fore-finger over the bumpy cactus-shaped handle of his spoon. "Was I a total jerk?"

Her eyes widened with surprise. "No."

"Then why are you making it so difficult for me to see my daughter? I mean, I did the right thing. We got married when you got pregnant. I might have been on the road a lot, but I never screwed around. I sent home a decent check."

"And you were never there." She leaned forward, her light brown hair swinging over her shoulders, her expression intense. "You missed most of Maddie's babyhood. Why do you need to be such a big part of her life now?"

"She's probably the only child I'll ever have." He paused, still fiddling with the spoon with one hand and wishing it was easier to articulate what he had to say—what he should have said a long time ago. Finally he just spit it out. "I never wanted our marriage to fail."

Jillian's blue eyes were solemn as she said,

"It would have anyway, Kade. Your heart wasn't in it."

He was stunned. Yes, his heart had been in it. He'd made a commitment and he'd intended to see it through—unlike his mom, who'd walked out on him and his old man when he was twelve. And he intended to be there for his kid—unlike either of his parents.

"I know about her," Jillian said in a low voice as she clasped her hands in front of her.

"Her?" Kade frowned and then moved his chair forward as another couple seated themselves at the table behind them.

Jillian lowered her voice even more. "I know that you left someone else to marry me."

Kade nearly dropped the spoon. "How?"

"I just asked. It was easy. People were happy to fill me in."

"Why didn't you tell me?"

"Why?" Jillian asked with a slight shrug of her delicate shoulders. "It wouldn't have changed things."

Kade shifted in his chair again when the waiter arrived with the tea. The man smiled politely as he set the pot between them, then quickly moved on to more promising tables. "Maybe we could have talked."

"Maybe. And maybe I was afraid of the truth."

"I never saw her after we were married," Kade said. "Never had any contact."

"Because of you or her?"

"I made a commitment to you and Maddie. I wouldn't have messed around."

Jillian stared off across the restaurant. "Maybe we could have worked things out if we'd talked, Kade." She looked back at him. "If we could have talked like this—which we didn't seem to be able to do." She bit her lip. "Think about it. This is probably the first time we've ever talked with all the barriers down." She paused. "I guess after hearing about…whoever she is…"

"Libby."

"Libby. I guess I wondered if you were seeing her on the road. And I thought that you had to resent being wrangled into getting married."

"It was my choice."

"*Did* you resent it?"

"Jillie." He reached out to take her hand, which was cold. "I made a mistake. If I resented anything, it was just that I'd made a stupid error and messed up my life. Your life. I never resented you."

"But you never connected with me, either. I thought that when we had the baby, it would cement the weak spots in our relationship." She gave a short laugh. "Isn't it grand to be twenty-two and oblivious to reality?" The smile faded away. "Have you seen Libby?"

"Yeah."

"So…are you working things out?"

"I doubt that'll happen. Libby is not the forgiving kind."

"Then you don't need her in your life," Jillian said, picking up the teapot and pouring hot water into both cups.

Yeah. I do. She'd been in his life forever and he wanted her there again.

"We have to come to an understanding about Maddie," Kade said gently, bringing the conversation back to the area he might be able to fix. "I want my time and I don't want to fight for it. Maddie needs to have a relationship with me, as well as with Mike. And you have to admit, I've been supportive of your relationship with him."

"I thought you were glad to have me out of

your hair." Jillian opened the tea bags and dropped them into the cups.

"I was glad you were happy, because that meant Maddie would be happy. Damn it, Jill, I know what it's like to grow up with an unhappy parent. I was abandoned by one."

She drew a deep breath in through her nose. "I always told myself that you had no idea how to be a parent because of that, but I think I've been wrong there. Maybe it's the reason you are a good parent."

"I pretty much follow the rule of opposites. If my father would have done it, I don't."

Jillian managed a laugh before her expression grew serious again. "I hope you'll still let Maddie go to horse camp. I shouldn't have brought that into the equation, but I did, and I want her to be able to go. My mom is excited to be watching out for her while she's there and…" Jillian gestured helplessly.

"And I'm willing to work around that. But I need my time with my daughter, too."

Jillian bit her lip again. "Mike has told me that I need to back off a little. That Maddie's being… smothered."

"I don't think you're smothering her, Jill. I think maybe you're a tad overprotective."

"I can't help it."

It was Kade's turn to smile. "I know."

LIBBY WOULD HAVE liked to give Blue some bute for the inflammation in his leg, but she wasn't going near him until Kade returned. She solved the screaming-horse problem by taking her mares to Jason Ross's place and putting them on pasture there. Jason had wanted to know the reason behind the move, but she'd done him enough good turns in the past that he didn't push when she sidestepped the answer.

Once he realized his mares were gone, the stallion settled in fairly well, limping the peripheries of his corral, occasionally leaning over the fence to threaten one of Libby's burros, who simply ignored him.

As skinny as he was, he was an awesome animal, with his black mane hanging well past the bottom of his neck and his tail practically dragging the ground. He had a stallion crest—a testosterone-induced thickening of muscle—on the top of his neck, but his head was fine, his chest deep. His distinctive crooked blaze contrasted sharply with a solid black head, and the rest of his body was pewter-colored. If his herd hadn't been located so remotely prior to the fire that destroyed their range, Libby was certain he would have been captured and adopted long ago—which wouldn't have been totally bad. If that had happened, she wouldn't have made love to Kade. Wouldn't be thinking about the effect he had on her.

She went into the house, kicked off her barn boots and padded into the kitchen in her stocking feet. So where was Kade now? Had he managed to get the job? She hoped so, because then he would sell and leave. He'd move closer to his daughter, as well he should. Didn't want to miss that childhood.

It bothered her, though, that he'd experienced parenthood and she hadn't. There was still time for her to do so, but it was ticking away.

She picked up the lanyard his daughter had given her. For no reason she could think of, she'd snapped it onto her horse-trailer key. As if she needed a reminder of Kade's kid. But Maddie had been so proud of those bits of twisted plastic, Libby hadn't had the heart to toss it once she'd gotten home. Pink and silver. Those appeared to be the child's favorite colors.

What had been her favorite colors at that age?

She tilted her head back, tried to remember. A normal person would be able to call her mother and ask. Libby's mother wouldn't have even remembered. She'd been too stoned throughout Libby's childhood.

Nine years old. She had a feeling her favorite color had been palomino. She didn't remember pajamas with cute motifs or anything like that. Just a room filled with horse stuff, where she could escape the indifference of her parents.

What kind of parents let their preteen daughter ride all over the desert alone? *Her* parents. Thankfully, she'd had Kade and Jason and Menace. She'd been just one of the guys. Until she'd fallen in love with one of them.

And gotten dumped on her ass.

CHAPTER TWELVE

KADE HAD BARELY GOTTEN home Friday morning when Kira Ross, Jason's wife, called, asking if she could stop by to see the ranch.

"I'm sorry for taking so long, but my son's been sick with an ear infection that kept coming and going and I had some family business to wrap up—"

"Hey," Kade said, "you're doing me a favor. No apologies necessary."

"Thanks. Then I'll see you around noon."

Kade drove over to Libby's, knowing she'd be at her office, and there he spent some time working with Blue. He managed to halter the stud and mixed some bute in with his grain, hoping that would help the swollen leg.

Then when he returned home, he walked around his property as he waited for Kira, taking inventory. The stone barn was good.

Marvin, the first Realtor, had told him that as if it was a huge revelation. The house was bad. He hadn't needed Marvin's opinion to see that. Fences—a lot of work ahead of him. The pastures—he hadn't even begun there.

What if he decided not to sell?

And why the hell was he having such a thought? If he didn't sell, he'd spend the rest of his life in a horse trailer parked next to the barn.

He had to sell. He wanted to be closer to Maddie. He needed a job as a backup for when Rough Out was done with him. Joe Barton's colt money was seeing him through now, keeping him in gas and groceries, but unless he trained at least four or five colts a month, he'd be living at the poverty level.

Plus, he'd never be able to erase the memories his father had branded into this place.

Kira showed up at twelve o'clock on the nose. She leaned into the backseat of her car and unstrapped a toddler from his safety seat, then hefted him onto her hip as Kade crossed the yard to meet her.

Kade smiled. "Jason Junior?" The boy had dark hair just like his dad, and really green eyes.

Kira smiled back as the little boy leaned

into her and then gave Kade a curious look from the safety of her shoulder, his fingers curling around a hank of her straight blond hair.

"Easy, champ," she said as she unfastened his chubby fingers, wincing in the process. "This is Matthew. Matt to his friends." Her eyes crinkled. "You're a friend."

"Hi, Matt," Kade said.

The boy buried his face, then peeked out, smiling coyly. Kade laughed.

"Where do you want to start?"

"The house," Kira said.

Kade took her through the house, expecting a round of utter condemnation, but to his surprise, Kira saw things that neither he nor Marvin had appreciated.

"Oh my gosh," she said. "These floors. They're solid oak."

"They're scratched to he—heck."

"Doesn't matter. Are these same floors also under the tile?"

"I don't know."

"Want to find out?" She put Matt down and then took a screwdriver out of the tool set Kade had sitting on the counter. "Do you mind?"

"Go for it."

She did, prying up one corner of a loose tile. Then a moment later she sat back on her heels, a satisfied expression on her face. "Yes."

"Good?"

"Very good."

"I was about to cover them with laminate flooring."

"I'm glad I got here in time."

And then there was the molding. And the ceramic doorknobs. She didn't seem to care at all about the patched hole in the living room where his old man had practically knocked Kade through the wall when he'd discovered that Blue was missing. The hardwood doors made up for it. As did some of the other architectural features that Kade had always taken for granted—or been unaware of, since they'd been covered with the old man's clutter.

"Now don't get me wrong," she said as they stepped back outside. "This isn't a mansion but, Kade, you have a lot of potential here. You could make this a charming home without a major investment, other than paying for the things you have to fix, anyway."

"Plumbing and electric?"

"Yes. And whatever you do, don't get rid of that big farm sink in the kitchen or the pedestal sinks in the bathrooms. Or the claw-foot tub."

"They're chipped and the tub's been painted."

"They can be repaired and restored. Trust me."

"All right."

"Leave the original faucets, too."

"Sure."

After touring the house, Kira looked at the pastures and the outbuildings. Because of her ultrafeminine appearance, Kade had been chauvinistic enough not to expect a lot, but the woman knew her business, right down to identifying a particularly noxious weed that he needed to eradicate. Now.

When Kade finally walked Kira to her car, Matt was asleep on her shoulder and her eyes were bright with excitement.

"You have work to do, but I can get you a decent price, Kade. The only thing is…I think you're looking at waiting months after you get the work done. These things take time. I mean, we can sell more quickly for a lower price, but—"

"I'm looking at months anyway."

Kira settled the sleeping toddler in his seat, then turned back to Kade. She pressed her lips together for a brief moment, then asked, "How are things with Libby?"

"Rotten." He wasn't even surprised by the question. For all he knew, she might have a bet riding on the matter. But somehow he doubted it. Kira seemed like a classy woman.

She twisted her mouth slightly. "Too bad."

"Why do you say that?"

"Libby's a lonely woman, whether she admits it or not." Kade was working on that surprising statement when she held out her hand. "I'm looking forward to doing business with you."

He took her fingers in his. "Likewise."

AFTER KIRA LEFT, Kade walked through the house one final time, thankful that he hadn't accidentally destroyed any of the features that Kira had found so valuable. He'd honestly thought that the floor was past saving. He'd been wrong. And although he understood the value of decent molding, he hadn't known that antique sinks were desirable commodities. Or that the beams of the house were spectacular.

The landline rang just as he was leaving,

so he went back to answer it. A husky feminine voice he didn't recognize said, "May I speak to Kade Danning?"

"That's me," he said briskly, wondering what the hell? Was a 900 number calling him?

"This is Jodie De Vanti. We met at my father's ranch."

The lawyer. "I remember."

"I have my father's contract drawn up and I thought that maybe we could meet over a drink and discuss it."

"Sure you wouldn't want to find a quieter place to do business?"

"My father and some of his friends are going to the bar in Otto for dinner. It's some kind of special food night. Ribs, I think. But I thought if we got there early, we could get a table to ourselves and I could show you what I've drawn up."

"We could try," Kade said cautiously.

"If you have any concerns we can deal with them there, and then you can get it to your lawyer. Is six o'clock all right? There shouldn't be much of a crowd then."

"That would be fine. See you there."

The woman had a lot to learn about the

local bar if she thought she was going to conduct business there on a Friday night, even at six o'clock, but Kade saw no reason to be difficult. She'd figure it out and he'd be able to get his contract to Sheri, who'd pass it on to her lawyer.

LIBBY WAS HAVING the first decent day at work she'd had in weeks. The office was buzzing because the gather that Ellen had professed to have no knowledge of had been postponed, pending a review by the state office. Apparently someone had informed the protest group Run Wild Run Free of the impending roundup and had provided information indicating that it was a questionable action. The group had managed to get an emergency injunction. Ellen was taking it personally.

Libby went about her job, smiling to herself every so often. When she did leave her office, Ellen ignored her—a sure sign that she knew who the informant had been but had no way of proving it. And Libby was certain Violet wouldn't rat her out, since Run Wild Run Free might need Libby's expertise in the future. They wouldn't always see eye to eye, but she and Violet had reached an understanding during their recent phone conversations. Libby hoped now that maybe Violet would hear her out before automatically protesting range management, and she, in turn, would make an effort to get accurate data to Violet. There were times animals had to be removed. And there were times when they didn't.

All in all it had been a satisfying day, and Libby did her best to enjoy it, since she knew the satisfaction would probably be short-lived. Plus, tonight was rib night, and Libby was going out with Menace to celebrate her coup. She liked ribs more than chorizos, and she was tired of kicking around her house alone. She needed a night out with friends who didn't set her on edge.

The bar wasn't busy when she arrived, but by the time she hooked up with Menace and they'd gotten their food the crowd was growing. She wasn't surprised to see Kade come in, since he had to be as sick of being alone as she was—and his place was a lot more depressing than hers—but she hadn't expected him to cross the room and sit down at a table with an elegant blonde she'd never seen before.

"Joe Barton's daughter," Menace informed her before she asked. "Spitfire. 1977. Primo."

Libby smirked to hide the fact that it didn't feel all that great to see Kade with another woman, especially one associated with Joe Barton and who drove a car that Menace obviously coveted. But Kade's life choices were none of her concern. She could have made them her concern, but…she hadn't.

She and Menace avoided the pool table, finished their meal, then decided to have one more drink before calling it a night. It was her turn to buy, and since Ginger, the stocky redhead who'd just bought the local hardware store, had joined them and Menace was suddenly oblivious to everything but her, Libby took it upon herself to go to the bar.

"Hey. Mustang Girl."

If the term "girl" hadn't stopped her, the tone of voice would have. Challenging. Not very nice. Libby turned to see the man who had spoken. He was standing about three feet behind her, glaring at her with his thumbs hooked inside an expensive horsehair belt. She didn't recognize him, but with his artificially faded jeans, pricy retro shirt and expensively styled hair he looked like a rich fraternity boy playing cowboy. Drunken cowboy. Libby turned back to the bar, since she didn't answer to Mustang Girl.

"What the hell were you thinking, letting those nags overgraze the range?" the man said, again from behind her.

She turned around and eyed the guy coolly. Yes, he was quite drunk. To the point of swaying slightly. "I guess I'm thinking you don't know what you're talking about."

He leaned forward, his boozy breath rolling over her face, making her grimace. "I know exactly what I'm talking about. Horses ruin range faster than any animal."

"Which is why the population is kept in check. Who are you?"

"I manage the Zephyr Valley. I'm the *foreman*." The guy slurred the word out.

"My condolences to your employer."

He muttered a curse, glancing over his shoulder, then back at her. Libby had the feeling he wasn't used to being challenged or insulted. She didn't give a damn. He'd started it, so she continued the lesson.

"The mustangs were on that land before your ranch had the allotments. I plan to see to it that they stay there."

The man's face went red. "Listen, bitch," he growled, taking hold of her upper arms. "You can stir up all the protestors you want—"

Libby twisted free, clenching her fists and wondering if it was fair game to slug a jerk of a drunk, or if Cal Johnson would arrest her for assault. She was completely shocked when the man was suddenly knocked on his ass by someone else.

Kade.

By this time another man was pushing his way to the front of the crowd, a man Libby recognized from photos in the news articles Stephen had showed her. Joe Barton. The owner of the ranch the booze hound had been defending.

"That's enough, Kade," Barton said in an authoritative tone.

Kade didn't even look at him. "You all right?" he asked Libby just as Menace reached her side and growled almost exactly the same words.

She nodded and Menace dropped a protective arm over her shoulders before scowling at Joe Barton and his crew. Kade ignored them all as he met Libby's eyes for one long, electric moment. Then he glanced over at Menace. Menace nodded, silently assuring him the situation was in hand, despite the guy rolling on his back on the floor.

Kade turned without another word and headed back to his table without acknowledging Joe Barton.

The older man watched him go, then reached down to help his foreman to his feet.

"I want that son of a bitch," the foreman growled.

"Leave it." Barton obviously meant it. "Are you all right?" he asked Libby.

"Tell your *foreman* that roughing me up won't change how many mustangs are on the range."

"He won't bother you again."

Joe went over to his employee and said something in a guarded voice. The man scowled and then left the bar. Libby turned to Menace. Ginger was hovering close.

"I'm fine," Libby said as they eased their way through the crowd. "Go back to your dancing."

"You're not fine."

"But I am going home." She'd had enough fun for one evening.

"I'll see that you get there okay."

"Just see me as far as my truck. You don't want Ginger to hook up with some other yahoo."

They left the bar by the front exit at the same time that Kade came around the corner from the rear. He walked toward them and Libby glanced up at Menace. "I want to talk to Kade."

"You want me to go back inside?" he asked as Kade approached.

"Yeah, I do." Libby patted his whiskered cheek, then headed toward Kade. Without a word they came together, simultaneously turning toward the end of the lot where their trucks were parked.

"You shouldn't have slugged him," she said as they walked. "I could have handled things."

"He's the type who would have hit you back," Kade muttered.

"Maybe," Libby said. They reached her truck and she unlocked the door. "But Menace was there. He would have taken care of business. Why'd you hit him?"

His gaze was intent when he said softly, "I think you know why."

Her lips parted, but she couldn't come up with any words at all.

"When we made love the other night, Lib, it wasn't because we needed to take the edge off."

"Then why?" she asked quietly.

"Because regardless of what happened, we're good together. We know each other. Inside and out."

She begged to differ, because if she had known him inside and out she wouldn't have been so utterly stunned when he'd cheated on her.

"I slept with you because I needed it," she insisted. "I, uh, wanted to get you out of my system."

"Did it work?" Kade asked. "Because it sounds like a dumb-ass idea to me."

"No. It didn't work," Libby said self-mockingly. And the idea *had* been dumb-ass. An excuse to indulge herself.

"So what does that mean?"

"It means I still like to sleep with you, but I'll never totally trust you."

"That's to the point."

"It's the truth."

"I think we should be together, Libby."

She held his gaze for a moment in the dim light of the streetlamp, feeling the electricity snapping between them. Then she opened the door of her truck and climbed inside without answering.

She wasn't exactly surprised when Kade followed her out of the lot in his truck. It seemed inevitable that he would follow her home. She didn't say a word when he parked next to her and got out, then simply walked up the path with her to her house, took the keys and unlocked the front door.

Libby went inside and Kade followed, shutting the door behind him. For a moment they simply stood facing one another in the dimly lit living room, and then Libby reached up and began to unsnap Kade's shirt, slowly, without looking at him. He put his hand over hers and when she glanced up, he kissed her deeply, his tongue pushing into her mouth.

She shoved his shirt over his shoulders without breaking contact, popping the rest of the snaps, greedily smoothing her palms over his skin. So hot. So burning hot.

His hands dug under her hair, lifting the mass of curls, then letting them fall as he framed her face, pulled her mouth to his again. And again.

Her hands were trapped between them, which was the only reason she wasn't reaching for his jeans. If she was about to make a mistake with Kade, it was going to be a gloriously huge mistake. She enjoyed sex with him and she'd let herself keep doing it. And since she expected nothing from him, she wouldn't be hurt when she didn't get it.

"I promise you, Lib," Kade murmured against her mouth, "we *can* be good together. And not just in bed."

Her body went still. "We're not a couple, Kade."

He raised his head, a stubborn gleam in his hazel eyes. "I thought we could work in that direction."

She simply shook her head. "And I thought you understood."

"Understood what? That the sex is hot, but that's all I'm getting?" Kade released her, his hands falling to his sides. "That you won't try to move past the anger?"

"Do you really blame me?"

"I did. Once." The words seemed to echo in the silence that followed.

Libby drew herself up, pulling her blouse back up onto her shoulders. "How so?" Because she was more than certain that she was the blameless party.

"Never mind."

"No. You are not pulling the 'man' act on me. How did you blame me?"

"Because you were the one who started backing off."

Her eyes widened and for a moment she couldn't speak, she was so annoyed. "You mean when I said we needed some time and you glommed on to it as an excuse to sleep around?"

"I…" He shook his head, obviously frustrated.

"What?" she demanded.

"I thought you were leaving me. I thought it was a done deal." He shrugged back into his shirt, leaving the front hanging open.

"I only said I wanted time!" she said incredulously.

"I thought you were cushioning the blow."

"I can't believe this." She took another step

back, away from him. "When have I ever cushioned a blow?"

"I felt abandoned, all right?" His voice rose as he said aloud what had been digging at him all these years. He'd thought himself weak for feeling that way, after he'd taken care of himself quite well for so long. "I felt as if the one person I could count on was no longer there," he said. "That you were slipping away. I was hurt and angry." And he'd looked for comfort in the wrong place.

Libby felt stunned. "I wasn't leaving you," she repeated.

"It sure as hell felt like it. There'd never been a time in my life when I couldn't count on you—until then."

"We were too young to get married."

A brief beat of silence followed and then Kade said, "Are we too young now?"

Her mouth fell open. "Damn, Kade…are you crazy?"

HE'D TERRIFIED HER. He could see that. After staring at him for another moment she backed up several steps, putting more distance between them, as if he could force her to get married by simply being close to her.

"Yeah," he said, snapping his shirt back up. "Crazy." He must be. Chasing a woman who'd never have him, who was too tied up in her own hurt and anger to let go.

And then she solidified his conclusion when she said defensively, "I was blindsided once, Kade, and a big part of me will always wonder if I'm about to be blindsided again."

"That's not fair, Libby. I can't undo what's been done. All I can do is move on. And for the record, I was blindsided, too." He went to the door. "I'll make arrangements to take Blue off your hands when I get back from Vegas. Probably Tuesday."

Libby didn't answer.

And he didn't say goodbye. He didn't say anything, because after telling her the honest-to-goodness truth, the truth he'd barely even admitted to himself, there was really nothing else to say.

CHAPTER THIRTEEN

LIBBY SPENT HER MORNING cleaning the barn and mucking out Cooper's pen. The horse's wire cuts and burns had finally healed to the point where she could release him into the pasture. He was celebrating by cantering in big circles, George and the burros running with him. Blue wanted to be part of the herd, but instead, he had to pace the length of his corral and back, joining in vicariously.

When the dogs leaped to their feet and shot out of the barn, Libby's heart skipped. Damn it, she had to stop reacting this way. She drew in a breath, stepped out of the barn and found Joe Barton's daughter standing next to a midnight-blue sports car—no doubt the Spitfire Menace coveted—as she petted Buster and Jiggs.

"Nice dogs," she said. Casually she brushed back a few blond strands that the breeze had blown over her expensive dark glasses.

"I like them," Libby agreed, wondering how it would feel to wear two-hundred-dollar jeans and a leather blazer every day. If she had such an outfit, she wouldn't be wearing it around Otto.

"I'm Jodie De Vanti."

"Libby Hale," she said, keeping the introduction brief as she waited to find out why on earth this woman was here. Jodie smiled and then took a quick look around, quite possibly comparing Libby's small ranch to her father's. Libby had heard that Joe Barton had sunk a lot of money into the Boggy Flat and she doubted her tiny spread could compare.

The horses were still circling the pasture, kicking and galloping. Every now and then Blue would give a don't-forget-about-me whinny.

"Your horses are certainly playful this morning." Jodie smiled in a way that made Libby decide not to underestimate the woman.

"I just let one out and they're getting reacquainted."

Jodie's expression became more business-like. "I actually came about the incident the other night. The one involving our foreman. I wanted to make sure you hadn't sustained any injuries."

"What?" Libby gave the woman an incredulous look. And then she saw what was happening. "Are you a lawyer?"

"Yes."

"And you thought that maybe I'd sue your foreman?"

The woman simply raised her eyebrows.

"And will the foreman sue Kade?"

"I simply came to make certain you hadn't been injured."

"I'm not sure," Libby said. "I'll have to wait a day or two and see if the whiplash kicks in." Jodie De Vanti didn't seem to see the humor in the remark. Good thing, because Libby hadn't intended it to be funny. "I guess the extent of my injuries depends on what happens to Kade."

The woman smiled then. "Excellent. I see we understand each other."

"Uh, yeah."

Blue whinnied again as the horses made another pass, drawing the woman's attention.

"He seems lonesome," Jodie said.

"He's recovering from an injury."

"Ah." She smiled coolly, then started back to her car. "It was nice meeting you, Ms. Hale."

"Oh, the pleasure is all mine."

JOE BARTON SHOWED UP at Kade's place in the late afternoon. Kade had been expecting him. His left hand was bruised from punching Joe's foreman, but other than that he had no regrets, except for going home with Libby afterward.

"You nearly broke Chandler's jaw."

Chandler? It fit. "He was harassing a friend of mine."

"Are you sure she's a friend?"

Kade gave the older man an appraising look, wondering what he'd heard. Nothing good, probably.

"In the future, Kade, I'd appreciate it if you didn't lay hands on my employees. Especially if we're going to do business together."

It was a low-key threat. But probably an appropriate one to Barton's way of thinking. He didn't want internal strife. Bad for business.

"Maybe your employees can leave my *friends* alone." Kade swung up into the saddle. "What was his beef with Libby, anyway?"

Barton raised his eyebrows. "You didn't ask her?"

Kade shifted his jaw sideways. He'd stepped into that one, but Barton took mercy on him.

"They had a difference of opinion about range usage."

"Must have involved mustangs." That was the only issue Kade could think of that would have gotten Libby so fired up.

"They *are* encroaching on my allotments."

"Not much feed out there. You can't blame them."

"Fewer mustangs, more forage for the cattle. The cattle enrich government coffers. The mustangs don't."

"They have their place in spite of that."

"I don't have a problem with mustangs. I have a problem with too *many* mustangs. If they're eating the grass, then the government doesn't get their grazing fees."

"And you don't get to sell as many cattle."

"Right." Barton didn't try to hedge.

Kade nudged the colt and he moved forward obediently. "I didn't know if we'd still be in business after I punched your foreman."

"We almost weren't," Joe said, leaning his arms on the fence.

"What happened?" Kade asked quietly.

"I figured you'd see things my way." Joe spoke confidently. Almost insultingly so.

Kade stilled. "Yeah?"

"Yeah."

Kade took a moment. Tried to talk some sense into himself. It wasn't taking hold. "So what happens in the future if I disagree with you on an important issue?" he asked. Like how his cowboys were treating Kade's friends.

"Keep it to yourself and we'll be fine."

"I don't know that I can do that, Mr. Barton."

"But you will."

Yeah? Kade dismounted and started unsaddling the colt. He'd never been able to resist a line drawn in the sand.

"Wait a minute…." Joe said, startled. "Is this it?"

"This is it. We're done. I'll expect to be paid for the days I've already worked."

"I have these colts sold with the understanding that you put thirty days on them."

Kade turned. "I haven't signed your contract and I won't work for a man who threatens me or my friends."

"She's your ex-lover, and from what I hear she's no longer that fond of you."

"She has good reason." Kade pulled the saddle from the colt's back and started for the barn.

"You need this job. I thought you were smarter than this."

"Well, now you know why I don't have a pot to piss in. I'm not that smart."

Goodbye, sweet deal. Now he really had to hang on to the endorsement. Nothing else to fall back on. Kade hefted the saddle onto the rack and then went out to find Barton leading the colt back to the corral.

"I'll send a man around to pick up the colts this afternoon. I'd appreciate it if you didn't assault him."

Kade nodded.

"Oh, and your friend… You may have just made her life a lot tougher."

Kade did not reply. It wouldn't do any good. But if Joe did anything to Libby, he would be one sorry man. Kade and Libby might never see eye to eye, but he wouldn't let anyone mess with her. He owed her that.

Barton got into his big, shiny red truck with the cab lights and the dually rear tires and started it up. Kade stood where he was as the man swung the rig around and then pulled out of the driveway.

Kade drew in a long breath, then exhaled.

He wiped his hands down the sides of his pants and went inside the house to tackle his father's room. The room he'd been avoiding since he'd returned home.

It was time.

KADE WORKED ON HIS dad's room until after midnight, bagging garbage and scrubbing things down. Getting the old man out of there. He finally went to bed, catching four hours' sleep before he had to get up and drive to Elko to catch the flight to Las Vegas, where he'd be photographed wearing Rough Out jeans. His buckles were packed in his carry-on. Everything else would be provided—clothes, food, drink, bed. And it wouldn't be hard to dig up some company if he so desired. Not a bad gig, and he knew how lucky he was to have landed it after the way he'd screwed up. He owed Sheri, but he comforted himself with the knowledge that fifteen percent of what he earned would be a nice thank-you for all her hard work.

The photo shoot went well, although it felt strange to be back in the "world champion cowboy" role when he no longer felt like one. The photographer was genuine, though, rather than an *artiste,* and Kade felt satisfied with the shoot when he returned to his room to shower off the sweat from the lights. They wanted to do one more session with another cowboy, and they asked if he could return in two days. No problem. More shoots, more money. And they were paying for the trip.

He went to dinner with Alan Prescott, the executive who'd pushed for him, the recovering alcoholic, and expressed his gratitude. "I'm a firm believer in second chances," Prescott said, "but I don't believe in third and fourth chances."

The message was clear, and Kade assured the man he'd be the kind of role model they wanted. And he would be just that. He'd done more hard living than he'd ever wanted to do, and it seemed that every mistake he'd ever made in his life had come back to bite him on the ass. He wasn't stupid enough to screw up this deal. Especially now that he was no longer starting colts for Joe Barton.

ELLEN SEEMED UNUSUALLY pleased with herself on Monday—a complete reversal of her Friday mood—which made Libby and the rest of the staff nervous. Even old Fred commented on it, and he never noticed anything. As a rule, he spent the staff meetings with his hearing aid turned off, sleeping with his eyes open, and the rest of the workday he played at being invisible. But Ellen radiated so much happiness that at lunch he said, "Queenie must have gotten permission to remove all the mustangs from the range."

Libby almost dropped her soda can. "Don't say that."

He smiled at her reaction, then shook his head. "I don't think she has that much clout. Yet. But she's a-workin' at it."

Libby made a mental note to check the job bulletins and see if anything was opening up, but she was aware that many upper-level jobs, such as the ones Ellen would be interested in, were known to prospective candidates long before they were advertised. Ellen might well have heard something through the grapevine.

Libby leaned back in her chair. If Ellen moved on, it was quite possible that she'd be out of here before she caused serious damage to either the mustang herds or Libby. But she was still uneasy, and she hated not knowing the full score.

Zero was in a talkative mood when Libby stopped by the feed store for dog food that afternoon, so she was late getting back to Otto. Rounding the last corner before her ranch, she was startled to see two official vehicles parked in her driveway— a white sheriff's SUV and the brand inspector's distinctive pickup with its light bar on top.

Her heart started beating faster.

No wonder Ellen had been smiling. It had nothing to do with her job and everything to do with Libby's job.

Libby parked in her usual spot next to the barn. Buster and Jiggs rushed to meet her, pressing their bodies against either side of her legs, eyeing the deputy and Trev Paul, the brand inspector, with suspicion.

"How are you doing tonight, Libby?" Trev's handsome face was set with a careful, impersonal expression. Libby had known him since high school—in fact, they'd had some fun times together during high-school rodeo— but right now he was every inch the law-enforcement officer, from the top of his dusty black hat to the toes of his scuffed Ropers. And she could see that while he wasn't happy to be in this situation, he had a job to do. He planned to do it.

"I'm all right, Trev." She nodded at the other man. "Cal." Libby pressed her lips together. This was not good.

Trev shifted his weight uncomfortably. "I need to see the brand inspections for all the animals on the property."

Almost on cue, Blue limped out of his shelter and started circling the corral.

"Sure," Libby said. She had no choice but to comply. "Come on in. Excuse the mess."

They stepped over the clutter of boots and shoes that had stacked up by the entryway, since Libby had been too busy that weekend illegally removing horses from federal land to tidy up. She went to her file cabinet and opened the second drawer, then removed an entire hanging file and led the way to the kitchen table.

"I no longer have some of these animals," she said as she began sorting through the file, pulling out folders of registration papers and brand inspections.

She didn't ask why they wanted to see her inspections, since she would have had to be pretty stupid not to figure out that she'd been turned in. And she was too honest to protest her innocence.

But in spite of that, she also wondered if she had any kind of brand inspection that would work for Blue. There was that one big gray gelding she'd sold a few years ago…but he'd had a brand. Blue didn't.

Trev sorted through the papers, pulling out the ones that matched the list of animals Cal had on a clipboard. When he had inspected the last piece of paper, he looked up at Libby.

"You're one short."

"Am I?"

Trev's mouth tightened. "Where'd you get the stud?"

"He's on loan from a friend." Libby casually put a hand on the back of one of the kitchen chairs, forcing herself not to fidget.

"Going to breed some of those mares in the pasture?"

"Obviously not," she replied impassively. "He's in poor condition and I'm pasturing him."

Trev placed the file folder on the table. "Then you should have a brand inspection if you have him on your property."

"Would you mind phoning the owner?" Cal asked quietly. "That way we can get the documentation we need."

"I can't." She wasn't about to lie to these guys, and she didn't want to implicate Kade. She wasn't going to do anything until she had some time to consider her best course of action. The one thought that kept pushing its way to the front of her mind was that she had a better shot at getting out of this than Kade did. She didn't want to jeopardize the endorsement deal for him. He'd make his money, sell the ranch. Then somehow she'd worm her way out of this and settle back to the way things were before, dating Sam on and off, growing old with her animals. Or maybe spending time in federal prison, depending on how this all played out.

"Lib?"

She looked up at Trev.

"I have to impound the stud."

"Good luck loading him," she said.

"I also have to investigate." Trev was serious. "You might want to do some thinking tonight."

"Who sent you?" she asked matter-of-factly.

"We got a call that a BLM employee had stolen a mustang."

"So did I," Cal said.

"Is anyone else involved?" Trev knew someone else had to be. Libby wouldn't have been able to capture and load a fifteen-hand stallion herself.

"I'm pasturing him for a friend. He's a domestic horse."

Trev and Cal exchanged glances.

"Damn it, look at him when you go out there, Trev. He's a foundation-stock quarter horse. It's obvious." Even though the animal was in poor shape, it was easy to see the classic quarter horse muscling, the long, sloping croup.

"We'll be taking the horse tonight. You'll be hearing from us shortly."

"Thank you, boys," Libby said scarcastically as she walked with them to the door.

"Honestly, Libby, this is nothing to mess with. It promises to be serious."

"Oh, I know that," Libby said. Just as she knew who had made those calls, and why Ellen had been smiling all day long.

KADE HAD BARELY been home an hour when the phone rang. He shifted his weight on the bunk, where he'd been reading, and dug the phone out of his jeans pocket.

"Kade? This is Cal. Cal Johnson."

"Cal. What's up?"

"We had to impound that stud at Libby's place."

Kade nearly dropped the phone. "What? Why?"

"I think you know why."

Damn.

"Trev Paul got a call saying that Libby was in illegal possession of a mustang. He had to follow up. Libby had no documentation, no brand inspection."

Kade cursed again. He shouldn't have let her keep the horse for him. The reasoning had seemed sound at the time but…shit.

"Did she tell you that he's my horse?"

"*Your* horse?"

"Yeah. My horse." Kade pressed a palm to his forehead. The last thing he'd wanted to do was drag Libby into trouble.

"Since when?"

"Since fourteen years ago."

"Come on, Kade."

Kade rubbed his hand over his face. Cal was younger than he was. He wouldn't remember a blue-roan stud disappearing. He'd been in grade school at the time.

"He's my horse."

"That's not what Libby says, and unless she changes her story, Ellen Vargas, that lady at the BLM, is going to skewer her."

"How do you know?"

"Because Vargas is the one who made the accusation."

Shit.

Kade swung his legs around and sat on the edge of the bunk. "How serious is this? Honestly."

"Serious."

So why was Libby covering for him? After everything that had happened…well, he wasn't about to let her put her neck on the line for him. The moment he hung up from Cal he dialed her home phone. No answer.

Kade jumped in the shower, shaved and dressed. Within half an hour of the call he was on the road to Wesley. He and Ms. Vargas, the BLM lady, were about to have a chat.

WORST-CASE SCENARIO, Libby figured she was facing time off without pay. Right now she was at the point where they had to prove she had a mustang, rather than an animal she'd bought without bothering to get a brand inspection. If it was the latter, she faced a healthy fine. If the former, if they could prove she had a mustang… Professionally, she was sunk.

It was Fred who delivered the bad news. "Are you crazy?" he asked in a growling tone. He looked like an angry hedgehog, with his bristly gray hair sticking out in all directions.

"How so?" Libby asked, her stomach tightening. She'd never heard Fred speak that way.

"Stealing a mustang?"

"He's domestic."

"Joe Barton has photos of him with the herd, and no one has reported a missing roan stud. Ever."

"You're wrong," Libby said. "He was reported missing fourteen years ago."

"Then I guess Trev's records don't go back that far," Fred said sarcastically. "And what the hell are you talking about?"

Libby glanced around. She wasn't telling her story in the office. She wasn't telling, period. She had a better shot of getting out of this than Kade did.

"Why would Joe Barton photograph the herd?"

"He took pictures when they were grazing down low last year, during the winter, trying to prove that the BLM had the numbers wrong, that there were more horses than there were supposed to be."

"I see."

"That, uh, roan stud is pretty distinctive, with the curved blaze and all."

Okay. Now she was in a spot of trouble. And that damned Jodie De Vanti had obviously seen the stud and put two and two together.

WHY IS LIBBY doing this? Kade could not figure it out. She'd made her feelings more than clear the last time they'd been together, so he couldn't understand why she'd taken the fall for him.

The U.S. Department of Agriculture was next to the Wesley BLM office and so Kade stopped by there first, hoping Trev was in. By some miracle, he was. He didn't see Libby's truck in the lot, but it was after four and she usually left around that time. Kade decided not to read anything into it.

"I'm here about Libby," he said as soon as he walked into the office. It appeared he'd just caught Trev after a day out, since his boots and jeans were covered with dust and his dark hair showed definite signs of hat head.

"What about Libby?" Trev asked.

"That's my horse you impounded, you know," Kade said.

Trev leaned his chair back, lightly tapping a pencil on his palm as he studied Kade— possibly searching for signs that he was lying.

"She said she was pasturing it for a friend," Trev responded after a few seconds, the pencil now still. "So…do you have proof of ownership?"

Kade rubbed a hand over his head. "Not

anymore. Hell, it's been fourteen years. Dad tossed out all my stuff when I left home."

"No secret stash of papers up in the attic?"

"Nothing." He was damned glad he had taken the few things that were important to him when he'd left—the photo of his grandpa, his box of buckles and the horse-show awards he'd won as a kid—or else they would have been in the trash, too. "You can DNA him. He has known bloodlines. In fact, he has some damned fancy bloodlines."

"That may prove he's not a mustang, but it won't prove you're the owner, and I think that bitch over there at the BLM will try to pin general horse theft on Libby, if she can't get her for stealing from the government."

"Shit." Kade picked up a rusty, old-fashioned horseshoe from Trev's desk, weighed it in his hand. He could use some luck right now. "Tell me the truth. Can Libby get out of this on her own?"

"You going to let her do that?"

"Hell, no. But I want to know what the worst possible outcome might be. Just in case I fail."

"If I were you, Kade, I wouldn't fail."

CHAPTER FOURTEEN

ELLEN VARGAS'S OFFICE was something. Nothing out of place, and there was a vase with some weird-ass flower sitting next to the highly polished telephone. Kade took off his best black cowboy hat when he entered the room.

"How may I help you, Mr. Danning?" she asked with a faintly belligerent smile, as if she knew exactly why he was there.

Kade was reminded strongly of that octopus lady in *The Little Mermaid*. He'd watched the video often enough with Maddie that he should be able to recall the character's name, but at the moment he was drawing a blank.

"The horse you're accusing Libby of stealing is mine."

"*Really,* Mr. Danning?" The belligerent smile still played on her lips.

Hagatha? No. Wrong story.

"Yes, really."

"Do you have proof? A brand inspection? Papers? Photos? Anything?"

Cruella? No.

"I released him fourteen years ago to protect him from my father."

Ellen Vargas gave a small cough. "Do you have any witnesses?"

"There are people in Otto who will remember the horse."

"Memories aren't enough, Mr. Danning. I want hard proof that this horse belonged to you."

Kade had no hard proof. As he'd told Trev, Blue's registration papers had long since been lost—as he'd had no need for them. There'd never been any photos taken of him and the horse. Who would have taken them? His father wasn't exactly one for keeping a family album. Libby hadn't owned a camera back then. And he'd only had the horse for a year before he'd released him.

"He's my horse. I let him go when I was sixteen. When I saw he was injured a few weeks ago, I decided to recapture him. Libby had nothing to do with it. I asked her to keep the stud for me because she had the facilities. She knew nothing about where I got him."

Ellen lifted her chin. Smiled. "Nice try, Mr. Danning. If there's nothing else?"

Kade put his hat back on his head, telling himself he hadn't expected a quick resolution to such a touchy situation. "Not right at the moment, Ursula." *That was it.* Ursula the Sea Witch. Maddie's favorite villainess.

"Ellen," she corrected.

Kade snorted and walked out the door. He was taking this bitch down, whatever her name was.

KADE STRODE TOWARD the rear exit, debating his next move. He'd go back home for now. Regroup.

"Kade." He stopped at the sound of Libby's voice. Since he hadn't seen her truck in the lot he hadn't expected her to be there, but now he turned to find her closing in on him. She was dressed in a white shirt and jeans, her long curls loose around her shoulders. "What are you doing here?"

"Taking responsibility for my actions."

Her eyes went wild. "Great. Just great." She brushed past him and shoved the exit door open. He followed her out into the parking lot. The door banged shut behind them.

"You're pissed I'm taking the blame?"

"Are you kidding?" Libby asked. "Ellen won't let you take the blame. I'm the one she wants to nail."

"I'm not letting you take responsibility for this." And why was she so damned angry?

"So basically I sacrificed myself for nothing."

Kade was startled into silence. He stared at her for a moment before he asked, "Why would you sacrifice yourself at all?"

Libby's cheeks went pink. "Because I'm a fool." She reached for the door, but he put his hand on it, holding it shut.

Her expression tightened. Libby wasn't used to being contradicted by word or action.

"The newspapers will glom on to this, you know," she said. "Ellen will see to it that they get her one-sided story. We're both going to look like horse thieves, and you're going to lose your endorsement contract."

"Why do you care?"

Libby opened her mouth to speak, then shut it again.

"You can't say it, can you? Can't admit it."

"What?"

"You sacrificed yourself for me because you care."

"Okay. I might care. But I can't trust you, Kade. And if I can't trust you, what have we got?"

"Bull, Libby. You're afraid to trust yourself. You're afraid to let go of the anger because it keeps you safe. Keeps you from having to take a risk. Keeps you from having to feel anything."

"I'm no coward."

"Yeah, you are. You're a coward because you refuse to admit the truth to yourself."

She drew in a long breath, then pushed his hand aside and opened the door.

"I'm done, Lib," he said before she could disappear. "I'm tired. I can't do this anymore."

"Neither can I, Kade." A second later she was gone.

Kade stared for a moment at the heavy gray metal surface as it swung shut behind the world's most stubborn woman, then walked to his truck.

He *was* done. He'd thought he could work

his way back into Libby's life, that after they'd captured Blue, made love, eventually things would change.

He'd been pretty damned wrong. If she didn't trust him, they had no chance together.

Kade had planned to drive straight home, but on his way out of town he had an idea and flipped a U at the city limits.

The *Wesley Star* was the biweekly paper that Kade had clipped newspaper articles out of when he'd been in 4-H and high-school rodeo. Libby had encouraged him to keep a scrapbook. In fact, she'd started the scrapbook for him, and then Kade had continued to add to it whenever she twisted his arm. There'd been one photo taken of him and Blue at a rodeo event. He wondered what kind of an archive the *Wesley Star* kept.

The receptionist was more than happy to show him to the basement where they had file copies of every newspaper they'd published, some on microfiche, some hard copies. Did he have any idea where he wanted to start?

Almost a half hour later Kade found what he was searching for, and his heart sank. Yeah, it was him and Blue, but the horse was in profile—his blaze didn't show. It could be any roan horse being led by a skinny kid.

So much for long shots.

All of them.

THAT NIGHT KADE called Jillian to ask if he could switch weekends. This didn't seem like the best time to have his daughter around, on the off chance he was going to be arrested for horse theft. Plus he had to fly out in another day. Back to Vegas for the shoot.

"What's happening?" Jillian asked and Kade told her. He told her everything.

"Wow," she said when he was done. "Maddie told me about the long fence in the desert. I had no idea what she was talking about."

"I probably shouldn't have taken her out there."

"Would you have caught the horse while she was there?"

"Hell, no."

"Then I don't see the problem. You went for a ride in the desert."

"Thanks, Jill."

"She wore her helmet, didn't she?"

Kade shook his head, smiling. "Yes."

"Maddie likes Libby."

"So do I, for all the good it does me."

"Sorry, Kade. I mean…well, I'm sorry everything worked out the way it did for you."

"I'm all right," he said lightly. "Three-time world champion bronc rider. Rough Out jeans model—for a while, anyway." They could easily cancel the ads before they went to print if he was involved in a public scandal because of Blue. He was fairly certain there was something in the contract that would keep him from seeing much money, too, if they did.

"Keep me posted, will you?"

"I will, promise. Would you mind explaining to Maddie for me when she gets back from practice? I'll call her myself when I get home from Vegas."

"I will. Good luck, Kade."

"Thanks."

He was going to need it.

"LIBBY, THERE'S SOMEBODY here to see you." Fred poked his head into her office long enough to deliver the message, then disappeared.

Libby's heart skipped. What now? A deputy

with handcuffs maybe? The only reason she was at work, instead of on forced leave, was that the investigation was still in progress. Innocent until proven guilty.

Two days had passed. Maybe it had just been completed.

She went out into the reception area, expecting the worst, but the only person there, other than Francine, was a pretty woman with light brown, sun-streaked hair. Libby knew instantly that this was Kade's ex-wife. She could see the resemblance to Maddie. The girl might have gotten her father's eyes, but other than that she was a clone of her mother.

"Libby?" the woman asked cautiously.

"Yes."

"I'm Jillian Kaiser."

"Nice to meet you," Libby said automatically.

"Yes," Jillian replied politely. "I wanted to talk to you about Kade."

Libby raised her eyebrows, wondering what on earth was coming. Not what she expected.

"Give him a break, okay?"

Francine glanced up, saw the expression on Libby's face and looked down again.

"I don't need advice from the ex," Libby said.

"Well, you're getting some anyway. Or if not advice, then information." Jillian swallowed and tilted her chin in a way that made Libby realize this was not easy for her. "I didn't know about you when I got pregnant."

"That's an excellent reason to give Kade a break," Libby said, moving to the far side of the room where Francine couldn't hear them, since this woman was obviously into straight talking.

"I didn't know about you for almost two years. Kade did his best to be a decent husband and father. But I always had this feeling he was going through the motions. So I did some digging and found out about you. I thought that maybe you were seeing Kade while he was on the road."

"Didn't happen."

"He told me."

"And you believed him?"

"Libby?" Her name sounded strange coming out of the other woman's mouth. "Has Kade ever really lied to you?"

"He lied by omission."

Jillian tilted her head. "You mean about me."

"Yes," Libby said shortly.

"He thought he was getting dumped." Libby blinked. She was surprised Jillian was aware of what she herself had just found out a few days ago. "He reacted. Once." Jillian adjusted the shoulder strap of her purse. "He didn't so much lie as rebel. And, Libby, he was twenty-one years old at the time. Think about it."

Oh, she was. And Libby also thought that Jillian might be petite and pretty, but she was no pushover.

"Kade and I made a mistake getting married for the sake of our baby," Jillian continued after a brief pause.

Our baby. Libby's stomach tightened, but she remained silent.

"We barely knew each other."

"Yet you slept together."

"I was lonely, and frankly Kade was one hot guy. And he was hurting. I thought…I thought maybe I had a chance with him. I was wrong, but we did end up with a beautiful daughter, so I guess it worked out in that regard."

Libby forced the corners of her mouth up, but inwardly she was fighting to keep her equilibrium. If she didn't care for Kade, then this…encounter shouldn't be sending alternating jabs of pain and jealousy though her.

Jillian let out a resigned breath at Libby's apparent indifference. She dug in her purse and pulled out an envelope, which she handed to Libby. "Kade gave Maddie a bunch of his rodeo memorabilia a couple of years ago. There was a scrapbook…. This was tucked into it. I think you may find it useful."

Libby glanced down at the envelope, then back at Jillian.

"My husband's waiting. I need to go." Jillian paused at the door. "Think about what I said."

"Sure." When the door had closed behind Jillian, Libby frowned at the envelope.

"Aren't you going to open it?"

She'd almost forgotten about Francine. She frowned at the receptionist, then lifted the flap and pulled out a single sheet of folded paper, her breath stopping as she realized what she was holding.

She slipped the paper back inside the envelope.

"Well?"

"Memorabilia, just like the lady said."

Libby tapped the envelope on her palm, then went back down the hall to her office.

Chastised by an ex-wife. Does it get any better than that?

She closed her office door and leaned her forehead against it. *Especially when the ex-wife is right.* She hadn't given Kade a break—even when he'd told her the entire story. He'd confessed the fears she'd never known he'd had, and he still didn't try to sidestep his responsibility. But she'd hung on tight to her anger because it was safer than taking a chance on him. Safer than trusting that he'd grown and changed. She'd hung on, even though she loved him. Until it was quite possibly too late.

"I'm done, Lib. I can't do this anymore" seemed to indicate to Libby that she'd waited just a bit too long before coming to her senses. So what now? What did a person who was not an emotional coward do in a situation like this?

She went for it.

And the first step was to face her fears—*all* of them—and beat them into submission.

LIBBY STOPPED AT THE USDA office as soon as she got off work. Trev was wearing his pencil-pushing clothes—a clean plaid cowboy shirt and new jeans—so she hoped he wasn't in a mood. Trev was not one of those guys who did well when he was cooped up. She knocked on the doorjamb before she walked in and placed Blue's registration paper on his desk. Trev frowned, then picked up the document. He studied it for a moment before setting it back on his desk.

"Well, well…Kade E. Danning owns a blue-roan stud horse."

Libby nodded. "Exactly."

He leaned back in his chair, a slight smile lifting the corners of his mouth, and Libby was glad to see the lazy amusement she'd always associated with Trev easing back into his expression.

"We'll pull a few hairs and run a DNA test to make certain he's carrying these bloodlines, but—" he pointed to the distinctive blaze drawn in black ballpoint pen on the printed outline of a horse's face "—I'd say this is pretty cut-and-dried. Let me make a copy."

"Sure."

When he came back a few minutes later, he said, "There's still the matter of releasing a horse into the wild."

"Maybe he just got away from us," Libby said with a half smile.

"And maybe there's a statute of limitations."

"Let's hope," Libby said. "Besides, we were juveniles."

"Juvenile delinquents, obviously," Trev said, handing back the document. "I'll be in touch with Kade."

"Thanks." She paused. "I have just one more favor to ask, Trev."

"What?" he asked cautiously. With good reason. Libby and Kade and Jason had gotten Trev into a few jams during high school. Nothing that left him with a record or any scars, though.

"Tell me where Blue is. Let me steal him for real."

"And I suppose you want help loading him."

"Not only that, I want to borrow your trailer."

"Why?"

"Because I screwed up bad with someone I love and I want to make it better. Even if I can't make that completely right, well, at least his horse will be back where he belongs."

Trev smiled slightly. "Just call me Cupid.

The horse is at my place. And I guess I can pasture him wherever I want." His jaw shifted sideways. "Unless it's at your ranch, since you're still the official suspected horse thief until notified otherwise."

"We're not taking him to my ranch."

Trev smiled for real, then pushed his chair back and got to his feet. "Three guesses as to where."

BLUE WAS IN THE CORRAL.

Kade sat behind the wheel of his truck for a moment and simply stared. It had been a long day, with two flights, two drives and a hell of a lot of explanation. Maybe he was hallucinating.

The stud whinnied then, and Sugar Foot obligingly came out from behind the barn where he could see her.

What the…?

He reached over the console and grabbed his duffel bag, then got out of the truck and started toward the corral. He was halfway there when he noticed that the door to the house was open. Not a little open, but wide open. He changed course and headed in that direction, cautiously approaching the door.

And that was when Kade got his second shock of the day.

Libby was standing in the kitchen, her back against the sink that Kade hated but Kira loved, her fingers resting on the enamel.

"Where's your truck?" he asked her.

"I got dropped off."

Kade would not allow himself to feel hopeful. Not again. She'd smacked him down enough that he'd finally gotten the message. She had to be here because of the stud.

"How'd you get Blue back?" he asked, trying to sound impersonal and not doing the best job of it. She was wearing the soft green shirt she'd worn to the bar the other night. And it wasn't buttoned much past her bra, showing a lot of creamy skin.

"Jillian found his registration."

Kade's eyes jerked from Libby's cleavage back to her face as his pulse pounded. "What?"

"She came to see me," Libby said, her fingers tightening on the edge of the sink. "Told me some…home truths. And she had the document. I guess it was in the rodeo memorabilia you gave Maddie." Libby picked up a tattered envelope off the counter and held it out. "Jillian said it was in the scrap-book."

Kade dropped his bag and moved across the kitchen to take the envelope, hesitating for a moment before he opened it and removed the single folded sheet. He didn't remember putting Blue's registration anywhere, but yeah, he could see where he might have stashed it in the scrapbook, not yet ready to let go of the memories.

He unfolded the brittle certificate carefully. *Steeldust Roman Blue.* Registered to one Kade E. Danning.

Once upon a time he'd held this paper and dreamed of a future in which he'd be a champion rodeo rider for part of the year and raise quarter horses the rest of the time. Blue would be his foundation stud, and together they would build an empire.

He swallowed and folded the certificate again before carefully sliding it back into the envelope. Funny how things sometimes worked out. But he and Blue were together again.

"Well...thanks." He pressed his lips together, trying to maintain his composure. He'd call Jillian as soon as Libby left. Thank her, too. Funny how they'd finally come to terms with each other after all these years.

"That's not all."

He met Libby's eyes, startled by the intensity of her voice. "What else?"

"You were right yesterday."

The words hung in the air for a few seconds, but Kade didn't say anything. He wasn't certain how to respond—yet.

Libby brushed a hand over her curls distractedly, focusing on the opposite wall as she confessed, "I am afraid of taking emotional risks."

"No kidding," he said gently.

"Do you blame me?" she demanded. "No one I've ever loved has really panned out. My parents weren't parents. And, well, you know what happened with us."

"Yeah. I know." His heart was beating faster.

She swallowed. "I love you, Kade." The words came out quietly, but fiercely. "I was so angry because you hurt me, but I still loved you. And that meant you could hurt me again."

She pulled in an audible breath and for a moment neither of them moved or spoke. Confession might be good for the soul, but it was hell on the nerves.

Finally he said, "Come here."

"We've got so much to work out."

"Come here."

Libby didn't wait for a third invitation. She went. She walked into his arms, leaned against his chest. And then she hung on tight as he slid his hands under her hair and over the soft fabric of her shirt.

"I won't hurt you again," he said against the top of her head.

"Yes, you will." He was about to protest when she said, "It's part of loving. But it's a fear I'm going to face—just like you're going to face this house."

"Excuse me?" He leaned back so he could look at her. Somewhere along the line she'd lost him. But good.

"We're taking back this house," she said. "We're going make it ours. I face my fears and you face yours."

He frowned, perplexed. "I already faced my father's room." And survived. It was over.

"Not in the way I have in mind." Libby trailed the tips of her fingers down the side of his face, setting his nerves on fire and making his groin harden even more—which had seemed impossible only seconds before.

She pressed her palm against his cheek and smiled for the first time that evening. "We're about to make this a positive-feeling place. One where you can walk in and smile because of the good memories."

He turned his head to kiss her palm, catching the subtle scent of perfume. The same perfume he'd bought her years ago. "I'm almost afraid to ask…"

Libby reached up to undo the top button of his shirt with a quick twist of her fingers. "Do you want to start in the kitchen or in the living room?"

Here. He wanted to start right here. But there was still one more issue, the most important one. And it had to be settled. Now.

He caught her hand before she could undo another button. Her blue eyes flashed up to his. "I know you love me, but I can't do this if you don't trust me. I can't watch you walk away again."

Her gaze did not falter. "I trust you."

He had to ask. "What changed?"

"Me. And you. I think we've both learned some hard life lessons…and…I think we both know how *not* to handle a situation."

"Damn, Libby." He kissed her then, pulling

her so tightly against him that her buckle dug into his hipbone. He didn't care. All he cared about was getting as close as possible to the woman he loved. Scars healed. He was living proof.

When he finally raised his head, he said, "As far as Blue goes, now that we have the registration you're off the hook, too?"

"Oh, I don't think so. I have plans to talk to the newspaper about the gather, but…" She shrugged. "That's not one of my fears. If I lose that job I'll get another—as long as it's where you are."

"I think we can arrange that."

"Good. Now…" She ran her hands up over his chest. "Which room, Kade? And no. You don't get to sleep in the horse trailer tonight."

EPILOGUE

KADE WAS NEVER GOING to love his childhood home, but Libby had been right. Thanks to her, the house did have a better feeling to it now that he had some positive memories to help replace the bad.

He'd returned the favor, giving Libby a few positive memories of her own—which was only fair since he'd been responsible for some of her bad ones. He'd also given her a healthy dose of moral support during her drawn-out battle with Ellen Vargas.

Libby might have been afraid of taking emotional risks, but professional risks didn't faze her one bit. She'd given as good as she'd got, and in the end, after more than a year, Ellen had accepted a transfer, making a lateral career move rather than advancing. Libby had been satisfied—apparently, by government standards, that was as close to retribution as she could hope to get. And by that time, she'd been happy simply to be rid of the woman and concentrate on different areas of her life.

Like the man area, which Kade appreciated. And the horse area, now that Sugar Foot and one of Libby's best mares were in foal to Blue.

"Dad!"

"Yeah, Maddie?"

"That photo guy is almost set up."

"Thanks."

One last shoot for Rough Out before they went with a younger cowboy, and then he was on his own. But he'd completed a welding course at the community college in Elko, and now he was working on a business degree so he'd know what he was doing when he went into business for himself. For now, though—it amazed him to think about it—Menace was his boss.

"Uh, Kade…" Libby stuck her head into the bedroom, fighting a smile. "They're almost ready for you to pretend to fix something in your indestructible jeans."

"It's not funny," he said.

"Yeah, it is," she said. "Funny and lucrative. Best of both worlds. And those people are coming to see the ranch tomorrow. Kira just called. She said these may be live ones."

They lived on Libby's ranch and spent a lot of time fixing up Kade's, and at this point he was willing to bide his time and see what happened in terms of offers for the place, wait for the best price. He no longer needed to unload the house and the memories as quickly as possible.

"So are you ready?" Libby asked.

Kade shifted his weight, stared for a moment at his wife. "Come here."

She shook her head. "No. I'll muss you."

He reached out and took her wrist, pulling her into the room and up against his chest. "I'll show you some mussing."

"Dad!"

"Later," he said huskily as he bent to kiss Libby. "I'll show you later."

Libby smiled. "It's a date."

* * * * *

*Celebrate 60 years of pure reading
pleasure with Harlequin!*

To commemorate the event, Harlequin Intrigue® is thrilled to invite you to the wedding of The Colby Agency's J. T. Baxley and his bride, Eve Mattson.

That is, of course, if J.T. can find the woman who left him at the altar. Considering he's a private investigator for one of the top agencies in the country—the best of the best—that shouldn't be a problem. The real setback is that his bride isn't who she appears to be…and her mysterious past has put them both in danger.

*Enjoy an exclusive glimpse of
Debra Webb's latest addition to*
THE COLBY AGENCY:
ELITE RECONNAISSANCE DIVISION

*THE BRIDE'S SECRETS
Available August 2009
from Harlequin Intrigue®.*

The dark figures on the dock were still firing. The bullets cutting through the surface of the water without the warning boom of shots told Eve they were using silencers.

That was to her benefit. Silencers decreased the accuracy of every shot and lessened the range.

She grabbed for the rocks. Scrambled through the darkness. Bumped her knee on a boulder. Cursed.

Burrowing into the waist-deep grass, she kept low and crawled forward. Faster. Pushed harder. Needed as much distance as possible.

Shots pinged on the rocks.

J.T. scrambled alongside her.

He was breathing hard.

They had to stay close to the ground until they reached the next row of warehouses.

Even though she was relatively certain they were out of range at this point, she wasn't taking any risks. And she wasn't slowing down.

J.T. had to keep up.

The splat of a bullet hitting the ground next to Eve had her rolling left. Maybe they weren't completely out of range.

She bumped J.T. He grunted.

His injured arm. Dammit. She could apologize later.

Half a dozen more yards.

Almost in the clear.

As she reached the cover of the alley between the first two warehouses she tensed.

Silence.

No pings or splats.

She glanced back at the dock. Deserted.

Time to run.

Her car was parked another block down.

Pushing to her feet, she sprinted forward. The wet bag dragged at her shoulder. She ignored it.

By the time she reached the lot where her car was parked, she had dug the keys from her pocket and hit the fob. Six seconds later she was behind the wheel. She hit the ignition as J.T. collapsed into the passenger seat. Tires squealed as she spun out of the slot.

"What the hell did you do to me?"

From the corner of her eye she watched him shake his head in an attempt to clear it.

He would be pissed when she told him about the tranquilizer.

She'd needed him cooperative until she formulated a plan. A drug-induced state of unconsciousness had been the fastest and most efficient method to ensure his continued solidarity.

"I can't really talk right now." Eve weaved into the right lane as the street widened to four lanes. What she needed was traffic. It was Saturday night—shouldn't be that difficult to find as soon as they were out of the old warehouse district.

A glance in the rearview mirror warned that their unwanted company had caught up.

Sensing her tension, J.T. turned to peer over his left shoulder.

"I hope you have a plan B."

She shot him a look. "There's always plan G." Then she pulled the Glock out of her waistband.

Cutting the steering wheel left, she slid

between two vehicles. Another veer to the right and she'd put several cars between hers and the enemy.

She was betting they wouldn't pull out the firepower in the open like this, but a girl could never be too sure when it came to an unknown enemy.

Deep blending was the way to go.

Two traffic lights ahead the marquis of a movie theater provided exactly the opportunity she was looking for.

The digital numbers on the dash indicated it was just past midnight. Perfect timing. The late movie would be purging its audience into the crowd of teenagers who liked hanging out in the parking lot.

She took a hard right onto the property that sported a twelve-screen theater, numerous fast-food hot spots and a chain superstore. Speeding across the lot, she selected a lane of parking slots. Pulling in as close to the theater entrance as possible, she shut off the engine and reached for her door.

"Let's go."

Thankfully he didn't argue.

Rounding the hood of her car, she shoved

the Glock into her bag, then wrapped her arm around J.T.'s and merged into the crowd.

With her free hand she finger-combed her long hair. It was soaked, as were her clothes. The kids she bumped into noticed, gave her death-ray glares.

They just didn't know.

As she and J.T. moved in closer to the building, she grabbed a baseball cap from an innocent bystander. The crowd made it easy. The kid who owned the cap had made it even easier by stuffing the cap bill-first into his waistband at the small of his back.

Pushing through the loitering crowd, she made her way to the side of the building next to the main entrance. She pushed J.T. against the wall and dropped her bag to the ground. Peeled off her tee and let it fall.

His gaze instantly zeroed in on her breasts, where the cami she wore had glued to her skin like an extra layer. A zing of desire shot through her veins.

Not the time.

With a flick of her wrist she twisted her hair up and clamped the cap atop the blond mass.

"They're coming," J.T. muttered as he gazed at some point beyond her.

"Yeah, I know." She planted her palms against the wall on either side of him and leaned in. "Keep your eyes open. Let me know when they're inside."

Then she planted her lips on his.

* * * * *

Will J.T. and Eve be caught in the moment?
Or will Eve get the chance to
reveal all of her secrets?
Find out in
THE BRIDE'S SECRETS
by Debra Webb
Available August 2009
from Harlequin Intrigue®.

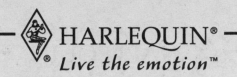

HARLEQUIN®
Live the emotion™

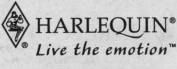

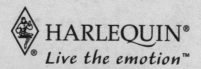